DARK TOURNAMENT

ELISA S. AMORE

AMORE
PUBLISHING

DARK TOURNAMENT

ELISA S. AMORE

Translated by Leah Janeczko

Through me is the way to the city of sorrow,
Through me is the way to eternal pain
Through me is the way to the ranks of the sinners. [...]
Abandon every hope, you who enter.

—The Divine Comedy: Inferno, Canto III
by Dante Alighieri

The Opalion

THE AIR SMELLED of sweat and blood. The dust stung our wounds as we awaited the Stage Director's next move. It was she who transformed the battlefield and chose our means of combat. We had fought barehanded and with weapons of all sorts, had maneuvered ourselves through mud and flames. They had even sealed us in a glass cage where sharp blades protruding from the walls threatened our every move. There was no limit to the number of challenges in this duel. It was win or die, a lethal game that would have only one Champion.

"Faust! Faust! Faust!"

It wasn't my name the spectators were shouting as I thudded to the ground on my back. It was my opponent's. I spat out a mouthful of blood, its taste filling my mouth, and locked my eyes on his. Encircled by a black mustache and goatee, his lips curled into a mocking sneer as the crowd cheered him on.

"No reason to gloat over an audience that changes sides so fast," I grunted. Not long before, everyone in the stands had been applauding my feats and shouting my name as I defeated an entire horde of Damned Souls to then battle a giant beast with pestilential breath. It had been fucking hard to reach that point. I had taken part in the Opalion often enough to know that the first two trials had been tougher than usual. Despite that, now I was right in the middle of the third one, the worst: the duel against the challenging Champion.

"Even the smallest victory deserves its moment of glory," he shot back with a grin.

"Well, they say settling for second best is a virtue. A shame it's not one of mine." I charged him and slid across the ground, knocking him off his feet. He was getting back up when the earth trembled beneath us and split open. We froze.

Within seconds the Arena had transformed yet again, leaving us only a few strips of land on which to do battle: concentric rings connected by walkways in the form of spokes scattered here and there around the circumference. I moved my foot away from the precipice and looked down. Nothing could be seen in the depths of the darkness.

"Get ready to take a dive, soldier," Faust warned me.

"I wouldn't count on it if I were you." I kicked up the staff that lay on the ground, grabbed it in midair, and twirled it over my head. "I was a pilot in the U.S. Army. I know how to bring down my enemies." I dealt him a powerful blow and he crashed to the ground.

A sneer appeared on his lips. "I was a firefighter. That doesn't mean I won't enjoy watching you burn." He leapt to his feet and tongues of fire burst from the chasm right behind me. The heat hit my back and I instinctively rolled into a front flip, gritting my teeth from the painful burn. I looked up and followed Faust's eyes to the Panthior, the platform of honor. It was his Amìsha—the Witch who had claimed him as her Champion—who commanded the flames. She was inside his head . . . and in his blood.

Only three of the ten members of the Sisterhood were watching the Games from above: Sophìa, the queen of the Underworld, in her ever-vigilant role as Stage Director; the Witch of Honor, who had earned the title by defeating her Sisters in what they called "the Hunt"; and last, the member of the Sisterhood who offered her own Champion to challenge the Witch of Honor's if he survived the first two trials. The two challenging Sisters assisted their warriors during the duel using black magic, while the Stage Director made the challenges increasingly more perilous. We were pawns in a deadly game in which the chessboard itself could do us in. As if that wasn't enough, the other seven Sisters watched over us in their guise as black panthers prepared to rip to shreds anyone who dared set foot outside the Circle. Seven ferocious felines spread out in a ring, their eyes trained on me. Their claws were lethal for those of my kind. One scratch was enough to kill us.

That was how the Witches spent their time at the Castle. That is, of course, when they weren't busy corrupting the minds of mortals on Earth by granting their wishes in exchange for a piece of their souls. No one could resist the Temptation, a promise of death that sooner or later led them to Hell.

Damned Souls weren't granted the luxury of battling for victory—they were tossed into the Arena as fodder for the Champions or the wild beasts captured during the Hunt. The more courageous Souls came to watch the Games from the stands set aside for them in the amphitheater. Opalion celebrations were the only occasions on which Sophìa opened the Castle doors.

Feeling the Arena's dusty ground beneath my feet reminded me that I was still in play, ready to fight. Faust and I had battled it out, chasing each other all the way to the last ring of land. The panthers prowled back and forth nervously, keeping watch over the areas assigned to them. They were eager to sink their poisonous claws into one of us.

The crowds cheered with surprise when I tackled Faust and pinned him to the ground, his face dangerously close to the borderline. "Not bad for somebody who's fighting without lymphe, don't you agree?" Elite Champions like Faust were allowed to drink their Witches' blood, known as lymphe. That was how the Sisterhood controlled them— and made them stronger. Tightening my grip, I shoved the staff against his throat. "I've heard the winner gets to spend a fiery night with his Amìsha. Not a bad reward."

"You have to earn the title before you can enjoy the privileges of a Champion." Using my staff as leverage, he broke free, hurling me away.

An arsenal of swords plunged from the sky, impaling themselves in the ground. Just in the nick of time I dodged one headed right at me. "Isn't that what I'm doing right now?" I grabbed the sword and our blades rang out as they clashed.

"Your tongue is as sharp as my sword. What a shame it won't help you win the tournament."

"I'm going to do far more entertaining things with it." I grinned at him, but a needle shot toward me and wounded my arm, wiping the grin off my face. "Ow! Weren't the flying swords enough?" I groaned. A second later I spotted a huge shower of needles zooming in our direction.

"Shit." I threw myself into a somersault to avoid them and glimpsed my opponent running in the opposite direction. He was trying to reach the walkway to the first ring of land, where an entire armory of weapons had appeared. I gave chase. I had to keep him from reaching it or beat him to it. Breathlessly, I raced after him around the last ring, dodging the needles shooting toward us. The panthers paced back and forth ominously, waiting for one false move. A series of spears suddenly sprang from the ground, forcing my adversary to slow down. I pounced on him, hurled him to the ground, and punched him repeatedly. He grabbed my face and shoved it back as though he wanted to rip my head off.

I heard a sinister hiss just as a needle pierced my ear. Faust laughed when he heard me curse. I bit down on his fingers and clenched my teeth until I tasted his blood in my mouth. He howled and let go of me.

Pulling myself to my feet, I touched the needle in my ear. "Actually, I might decide to keep it. Bet it looks good on me." Just then another series of needles struck my bare chest. "These, maybe not." I gripped them all in my fist and threw them to the ground, returning my attention to my opponent.

Time seemed to freeze along with our gazes, locked on each other. The needles had stopped, the spears had withdrawn into the ground, and the audience was holding its breath. It was just me and Faust now, ready to find out who would become the new Champion.

It was time to put an end to the duel.

He shot off so fast I couldn't defend myself when he

kicked me square in the back. He tried to attack once again, but this time I warded off the blow and began to punch him over and over, forcing him to back toward the edge of the chasm. Faust was a tough guy. Maybe casting him into the void really *was* the winning strategy.

"Only wusses attack from behind. Hasn't anybody ever taught you that?" I reproached him.

"To be honest, I learned it from you." His foot slid across the ground to the edge. I had him trapped. Gloating, I smiled. "See you on the other side."

Faust smiled back at me. "Pilots fly first." He grabbed me by the shoulders and with an amazing leap front-flipped over my head, inverting our positions. I ducked to avoid his punch, barely avoiding losing my balance. This time I was the one dangerously close to the edge. I caught his leg mid-kick and he spun around in the air to break free.

The crowds were in raptures over our dark dance.

"What, were you trained in a circus?" I inched forward just enough to be out of the danger zone and resumed the battle more aggressively than ever.

"This place is the most freakish circus there's ever been. Haven't you noticed that yet?" I shrugged. He wasn't all wrong.

A spear materialized not far away. It was my chance. I took a running start, slid across the ground, and snatched it up, but instead of hurling it at Faust I charged him. "You're right. Pilots fly first." I planted it in the ground and flew through the air, kicking him in the face with both feet.

"Drake! Drake! Drake!"

I turned to the audience, bowing. "I see you've come back to your senses."

Fast as a whip, Faust's legs jerked me down and I toppled onto him. "Have a nice flight, then," he shot back, grinning. He planted his feet on my abdomen and with a powerful shove sent me sailing over his head.

I didn't see it coming. The crowd gasped in shock. When I spun around, a panther pounced on me, her golden eyes sharp as those of a serpent.

I had crossed the line.

Her roar silenced the stands as her razor-sharp claws sliced through my chest. The poison set my veins on fire and a blinding agony clouded my brain. I heard the horn announcing the end of the tournament. Then everything went dark.

Game over.

1

AFTER THE FALL

I was once a Subterranean—a Soldier of Death—until Death claimed me and cast me into Hell, the only place from where there is no escape. Neither alive nor dead.

When I lived on Earth my mission was to redeem mortal souls and take them to Eden. Down here there was no one to save, so I figured I might as well enjoy my stay at the Castle. Sure, the hangover after every defeat in the Opalion was a real pain, but with time I got used to it.

The Subterraneans who didn't rebel were treated a whole lot better than the prisoners. I'd heard their screams coming from the Torture Caverns. What good would it do me to remain locked up, being tortured? That was why I'd gritted my teeth and agreed to be subjugated. In exchange, the Witches gave me more breathing room, more freedom.

The other alternative was to run away, which was out of the question, not to mention an insane idea. Who knew what ferocious creatures were lurking out there? There had to be a reason they called it Hell and I had no intention of finding out what that reason was.

The battles were a whim of the Sisterhood, the harpies who ruled the Underworld, and I had been battling for one of them. The rules at the Opalion were simple: fight for your Witch or die for her. Unfortunately for us, we Subterraneans were immortal. That was why they chose us for the Games. On Earth their lethal poison was the only weapon capable of annihilating us, but once in Hell there was no place else for us to go. Tournament after tournament, death after death, I was still condemned to Hell. Only Oblivion could put an end to everything, but that was a luxury very few were ever granted.

Feeling water choking me as I came to, I opened my eyes and jerked my head above the surface. I was in one of their healing vessels, pools of regenerating water carved into the rock walls. This was where they brought Soldiers after battles. The real magic was that the water didn't seep out of the vertical chamber.

"Welcome back to the living." The image of the young woman in front of me went blurry and then grew focused again. Lenora, if I remembered right. Her big green eyes smiled at me kindly, unlike those of her friend Khetra, who looked annoyed.

"Easy does it, Soldier. You haven't fully regenerated yet." Khetra pushed me back in by the shoulders so I grabbed her wrists and, to distract her, planted a kiss on her lips. They were Mizhyas, the Witches' maidservants. The form-fitting outfits they wore looked so sexy on their toned, curvaceous bodies. Brown, like their short fur boots.

She broke away, indignant. "You're as insolent as ever." She had a fair complexion and red hair, and was adorable when she pouted—that was why I always tried so hard to irritate her. Lenora was shyer but just as attractive, with her blond hair and Mizhya tattoo that made its way from her shoulder down to her breasts—I had personally verified that. Every Mizhya in the Castle had a tattoo somewhere on her body. They were all really artistic, all different, almost as though they were brands distinguishing each of them.

I laughed and pulled myself out, dripping wet and stark naked. "I already feel like I'm in great shape. What do you think?" I asked a third Mizhya whose name I couldn't remember. She must have been new. I winked at her and she tossed me a towel to cover myself.

Instead, I draped it around my neck. The water in the vessel reflected my tanned image. As a good soldier I had always shaved my head, but in Hell my hair had grown so long I had to tie it up in a ponytail. The tattoo of the Subterraneans that wound down my left arm kept me from forgetting who I was. My cuts and bruises had disappeared, leaving behind only the scars from the poison. Not even when I fought in the army had I collected so many of them. Not that I'd spent much time on the battlefield, given that I'd died when I was only twenty-three. Some girls even found them sexy, especially the two lines that cut through my eyebrow.

Khetra grunted. Of them all, hers was the name most firmly branded in my memory, and not only that. She knew how to play erotic games with her whip that were hard to forget. I didn't grant her exclusive rights to me, of course. I was definitely too much for just one lady. After all, I was in Hell. My soul was already good and damned. What worse could happen to me?

"Lenora, go call the mistress and tell her the Soldier is back," she said.

"What's the rush?" I grabbed the blond's wrist to stop her, but Khetra instinctively reacted, freeing her friend.

"Drake, do you want to get us killed?!" The Mizhya looked around, on her guard.

"Don't be jealous, Ginger. I didn't mean to neglect you. We can all have fun together."

Mine was a dangerous game, I was well aware. That was why I found it so amusing. The Mizhyas' lives, though, were way more at risk than mine. No enchanted pool of water could bring them back if they died. They weren't immortal like Subterraneans were. They were Damned Souls recruited in Hell to serve the harpies.

"You'd better not attract too much attention, otherwise we'll sell you out the first chance we get," Lenora said.

"Come on, keep me company for a while until I recover. It was a really rough tournament." I played with the little braid that dangled in front of her ear. That too was a distinctive sign. There wasn't an Amazon at the Castle who didn't have at least one braid, including the Witches.

"The prisons around here aren't a good place to hang out. You'd better toe the line or not even you will meet with a happy end."

"Kreeshna asked to be notified when you woke up and

that is what we're going to do," Khetra added coldly. Then she shot me a little smile. "I understand her impatience. I bet she wants to punish you again. After all, your tongue is more poisonous than her panther claws. Her serpent will put you back in your place."

Kreeshna. I hated faking being subjugated to her. She'd been after me since I'd transformed and had tried to wear down my resistance, but I had never succumbed to her. Now that I was here, what alternative did I have? At least at the Castle I could entertain myself with the Mizhyas. They were friends, and a rather amusing pastime to boot.

Reaching out, I grabbed Khetra's ass and pulled her toward me. "I know a place where I could put *my* serpent. What do you say?" I asked, grinning.

She twisted my wrists and a second later I found myself on my knees, my arms pinned behind my back and her knee shoved up against my spine. Sometimes I forgot the Mizhyas were trained to kill.

"Ow! If you don't feel like it, just say so. How about later?" Khetra shoved even harder. "Okay! I get it! I'll take that as a no. Would you mind easing up a little? My arm's still sore!"

"I could try to rip it off you. That would solve the problem."

"Hey, if it turns you on," I said playfully, and finally I heard her laugh behind me.

Her breath touched my ear. "In the stables of the East Wing, after the horn sounds the beginning of the Hunt. Lenora and I will be standing guard on the tower, so try to get yourself back in shape for both of us."

I smiled, already aroused by the thought. They always played hard to get, but deep down they had just as much fun with me as I had with them.

"Who's having fun without me?" a voice thundered as someone made their way into the caverns. *Kreeshna*.

Khetra shoved me away and bowed before her mistress. "I was keeping this Soldier in line, my lady."

"Exactly," the Witch pointed out, coming closer. She spread her arms and waited until her maidservants had undressed her. "Go. Leave us alone."

The Mizhyas bowed again and I winked at them. Lenora hid a smile as they slipped away.

"You weren't good enough in the Arena today," Kreeshna told me reproachfully, immersing her naked body in a little cascade of water that flowed from the rock. Her chocolate-colored skin glowed with golden reflections, her dark hair braided to one side. I walked over to her and her perfume was enough to leave me in a daze. Part of me hated that vulnerability, but I had to play along if I wanted to maintain control.

I stroked her neck with my nose. "My opponent was fighting with the power of Witch's blood in his body."

"If you want my lymphe you'll have to earn it, Child of Eve," she said sternly. "Children of Eve" was the name the Witches used for those of my bloodline. We Subterraneans were descendants of the children Eve had hidden from God since she hadn't yet purified them in the sacred river. For this offense, we were condemned to ferrying mortal souls to Eden—one of the reasons Witches and Subterraneans were mortal enemies. The Witches wanted those souls for themselves.

"I thought I was already doing that," I whispered against her lips. Every Witch claimed a certain number of Subterraneans for herself, but she chose only one of them as her Champion. Then she would offer him her blood so he would battle to the death for her. Kreeshna had never designated me as her Champion, though she had claimed me. This made her my Amìsha—and me her slave. One of the many.

She continued to send me out to do battle despite the fact that I had never won an Opalion. I didn't have a chance against the other Witches' Champions who had been allowed to drink their lymphe. No other substance could rival its extraordinary effects. During the Games, the Witches manipulated their Champions by means of the infected blood running through their veins. They gave them more strength, made them more cunning . . . they controlled them. Anything, as long as it meant triumphing over the other members of the Sisterhood. It was all just one endless competition among them.

The Witches' blood was their most powerful weapon for subduing us, and we yearned for even a single drop. A taste of paradise, they said. Some of her Sisters offered it more readily, even to prisoners, when they wanted to have fun. But not Kreeshna. I couldn't figure out why she kept sending me out onto the battlefield without it. She was always asking me to make more of an effort, to fight more ferociously if I really wanted her lymphe. But how could I win without the help of her power to begin with?

Once in a while the Sisters challenged each other in the Kryadon—the Hunt—and rode their winged steeds as they tracked down the strongest warriors spawned in Hell, creatures to recruit for the Opalion. It was nothing more than preparations for the Games, a challenge, like everything else that had to do with them.

It was impossible to hide from the Sisterhood. Some of the Damned even saw being recruited for the Games in the Arena as a privilege. They considered it a good way to die.

The Kryadon was a point-based competition. The Sister who brought home the most dangerous plunder won the title of Witch of Honor and opened the Games in her honor at the Arena, where she could show off by sending in her chosen Champion to fight. Battles excited them. If he was worthy and won for her, incredible pleasures with his Amìsha were in store for him. The Champions had to realize that winning in the Arena had its advantages. The Witches were lusty creatures, so Opalions were held often.

I had never really gone into battle for Kreeshna's sake. I did it because it was fun and because it was the best way to pass my time at the Castle, apart from entertaining the Witches' maidservants, of course. They were masters at the art of satisfying Subterraneans' needs. The Witches used us to quench their own thirst. Somebody else had to think about us.

My hand slid down the Witch's body, brushing against her breasts. It slid further as the Witch closed her dark eyes, yearning for pleasure. I ran my tongue down her cleavage and she dug her gold-painted fingernails into my shoulder ecstatically. Licking her was pure torture. Satisfying her without anything in exchange was my punishment for not winning. A bittersweet punishment.

A hiss made me freeze.

Recognizing the sound, I stayed perfectly still. The Witch's serpent coiled sinuously up her chest, his dark eyes staring at me threateningly. Each Sister had her own Dakor, and together the two of them formed a single being. Kreeshna smiled and her pupils lengthened, becoming identical to those of her creature. "Over the centuries, I have always chosen my Champions with great care."

"I can't win a tournament if I'm fighting without lymphe."

"Training is the key to victory."

"What, is it because you still don't think I'm worthy? Doesn't it bother you, losing in front of your Sisters? Competition is everything for you guys, you've said so yourself."

"A defeat learned from today means a great victory accomplished tomorrow. When you have a lot of time on your hands you can afford to look at things in the long term, don't you think?"

"So what are your long-term plans for me?"

"That's for me to know and you to find out, Soldier." The Witch stroked my head and grabbed my hair, biting my neck. "A Champion needs to demonstrate his strength *before* being chosen. And he needs to be faithful to his queen above all else," she whispered.

I stiffened. Had she penetrated my barriers and dug around in my mind? The Witches were masters at reading people's thoughts, but I kept mine well protected. I would have to be more careful.

"What makes you think I'm not faithful to you, my queen?"

"I know you well, Soldier. I knew you long before you ended up here." The Witch ran her sharp fingernail down my naked chest over my heart, leaving a red streak behind. I gritted my teeth as the poison burned my blood. Her face transformed, taking on the appearance of someone I knew well. I flinched, but quickly tried to hide how shaken I was. It was Stella, the fiancée I had lost long before.

"Even if you continue to push me out of your mind, I know she's still in there."

I balled my hands into fists. The Witch had often morphed into my long-lost love, to subjugate me completely, maybe. Or to torture me, because despite everything my grief over losing Stella had never faded. Though I continued to surround myself with girls during the many years I'd spent on earth after my death in World War II, no one had ever filled the void she'd left. Stella had died decades earlier, also slaughtered during the war.

"That's it, that's the fire I'm looking for," she went on. "I see it in your eyes, feel it flowing through your veins when you look at the face of this mortal woman." With her nails she traced a path over the mark of the Subterraneans on my arm. "This is the ardor a Champion feels for his queen."

Overcome by the sensations, I moved closer to the Witch and kissed her, pretending it really was Stella. Kreeshna was right: heat burned in my chest at the thought of actually having her there with me, but it was just a lie. Stella was a distant memory that I had never let go of. Again, I clenched my fists. I had to be careful. The Witch had bedazzled me, but I had to cling to reason and not lose control unless I wanted to end up a prisoner in one of their dungeons. With them, everything was a test.

I broke away from her and looked her steadily in the eye. "You don't need to change your appearance to bring me closer to you. There's no creature more beautiful in all the kingdom," I lied. "There might have been a time when I rejected you, but now I have no desire other than to serve you."

The Witch bought my bullshit and broke the spell. Her appearance changed back to normal. "I'm so happy you succumbed to me. It was a wise decision."

I kissed her shoulder as fiery rage burned inside my chest. "You've taken my soul, you know that. I'm yours. Let me fight as your Champion."

The Witch relaxed at the touch of my hands on her body. "You're definitely moving in the right direction." Kreeshna moaned, her longing evident, then put her hand on my head and pushed me down. She rested one foot on my shoulder, opening herself to my kisses. "Don't stop. Don't run from me."

"I would never run from you, my lady," I told her, fawning.

The steam rising from the water surrounded us, filling the air with a spicy aroma. I hated her but loved her at the same time, addled as I was by her power. It was the promise of her blood that had that effect on me. It would give me my strength back. Maybe it would even give me back the powers I had lost when I arrived there. The only problem was that I risked losing myself in her. I shook my head, trying to liberate myself from her spell. By surrendering to Kreeshna I had allowed her to enter my soul.

A ghastly sound echoed off the walls of the grotto, making a swarm of black butterflies flutter away from the ceiling and scatter through the cavern. It was the Sisters' horn. One of them was announcing the start of the Kryadon.

Lenora rushed in, out of breath, to tend to her mistress, who pushed me away as a suit of armor materialized on her shoulders and head. The metal helmet looked like a prolongation of the tattoo that was spreading over her face. It made her look like a butterfly, especially the pointy antennas.

"Make do with the privilege of serving me, Child of Eve," she replied. She grabbed the weapons the Mizhya was holding out to her: two short-handled whips, their leather straps trimmed with nails. A flick of her wrist and they burned into my skin, forcing me down, my palms on the ground. I gritted my teeth to keep myself from reacting. Her serpent hissed and lunged toward me. Maybe the beast could sense the hatred I was emanating.

"Yes, my lady."

The rest of the armor formed over the Witch's body. "We'll meet again soon, Child of Eve. I'm going out to win the Hunt. That way you can die in the Opalion for me . . . yet again," she said provocatively. *The sadist.* With that, she disappeared.

"I can't wait," I muttered sarcastically. My eyes met her maidservant's. She looked sorry for me.

How much longer would I have to keep up the charade? Was it really worth it, being treated like a filthy slave? Sooner or later I would have my revenge on Kreeshna. All I needed was to feed off her blood. Then I would annihilate her. Her and all her Sisters. I had to resist.

I smiled to myself.

Until that moment came, there were two young ladies waiting for me in the East Wing.

2

THE CASTLE WALLS

I sneaked up the long, narrow stairway leading to the roof of the tallest tower. It hadn't been hard to go unobserved. The Witches had all left to take part in the Kryadon and the only people around were Mizhyas and other claimed Subterraneans. I had even crossed the inner courtyard, where an army of Mizhyas were training in what looked like an actual battle. From there, various wings of the Castle, joined by tall, ominous-looking towers, could be reached. During the Games, the courtyard morphed into an amphitheater and the magic began. Though the flooring inside the Circle constantly changed, growing smaller and transforming itself, their macabre symbol was always present at its center, interwoven with that of the Subterraneans like an ancient threat. It was a sign of their power and their supremacy over our race.

There were ten Witches at the Castle, all as sexy and

gorgeous as they were evil and deadly. Camelia was the most eccentric and sensual, with hair that often changed color; Nausyka, her silver hair streaked with black, was the most capricious; Anya the wisest. There was Zafirah, with violet eyes and short, curly hair; Nerea with yellow eyes and blond hair spotted like leopard fur; Zhora with big green eyes; and Bathsheeva, the golden-eyed warrior with a long ebony ponytail. Each of them was pure evil. Then there was Sophìa, the Empress of the Underworld. The devil in person, to be exact. I hadn't run into her very often. She was a bizarre, eccentric creature. Even more than her Sisters, I mean. She wore sumptuous, close-fitting black gowns that suddenly changed their appearance since they were made of live butterflies, her precious black Souls. When she wasn't present, her Specter took command of the Castle. That role belonged to Devina and I had no doubt as to why. She was the most malicious Witch of all the Sisters, an even bigger bitch than Kreeshna. The devil's perfect right-hand woman. Rumor had it that Sophìa loved to stay in her secret refuge for long periods of time, sorting through the Souls that the Witches had collected on Earth during the Reaping. The Souls arrived at the Castle in the form of black butterflies and the Empress divided them up based on their sins, giving each the punishment they deserved. Then she released them, leaving them to the cruel mercies of Hell. Only the strongest survived the trials of the Copse.

Nope, I had no intention of finding out what was out there. I was fine right where I was.

Whenever Kreeshna wielded her superiority over me, the blood boiled in my veins and I wondered whether I was doing the right thing. Then I would try to focus on the advantages, like I was doing right now. I would rather pretend to be subjugated than rot in a prison cell. The cool air atop the tower confirmed that thought. It was like finally emerging from a catacomb. It felt like freedom.

"I was wondering when you'd show up."

I turned toward the voice. Khetra was above me, sitting on one of the black stone battlements crowning the tower. We were by the stables reserved for the Sauruses, the winged lions that looked kind of like black dragons. The Witches rode them through the skies of Hell. The massive stalls were empty now, which was why the Mizhyas were standing guard. Normally the Witches' steeds watched over that section of the Castle.

I leaned over the edge to see what was on the other side. The tower was so tall nothing could be seen in the darkness of the void below. "Guess you're not afraid of heights."

"Looks like you are, though. You're pretty pale." Khetra jumped down and landed next to me. She ran her fingers through my hair, undoing my ponytail, and kissed me passionately.

"You don't waste any time," I murmured with a grin.

"I want to take what I want before my mistress comes back and chops off my head."

I pushed her against the wall and this time I was the one who kissed her. "You like danger. You're lucky because I like it too."

"You throw a party and don't wait for all the guests to arrive?" Lenora's head peeked over the Castle wall. She climbed over it nimbly and jumped down beside us.

"How the hell . . . ?" I murmured, stunned. The tower was incredibly high. She couldn't have climbed it with her bare hands. The Mizhya smiled and threw two daggers in my direction. They lodged in the wall behind me. I admired them, finally understanding: they had hooks on them.

"I wasn't trying to cheat you out of anything. We were just warming up," Khetra told her.

I pulled one of the daggers from the wall and studied it. "Is climbing tall, perilous castle walls your favorite pastime?"

She snatched it out of my hand. "Patrolling the Castle walls is my duty. As for pastimes, I prefer far different things." She went to Khetra and kissed her ardently.

I smiled. "The party's getting more exciting." Both the Mizhyas claimed me, pulling me towards them by my waistband. Two aroused girls risking their lives for me. Like I said, the Castle wasn't such a bad place after all.

Lenora's eyes didn't leave mine as she pulled another dagger out of a sheath strapped to her thigh. Man, was she armed.

"Babe, I like danger, but what do you mean to do with that?" I asked with alarm.

"Don't worry, I come in peace." She slid her fingers into the now-free sheath and pulled out a long vial. It was metal, so there was no way to see what was in it, but I would've bet my balls it was red.

"Is that what I think it is?"

She nodded. "I know an apothecary. He assured me we'd have a good time."

It wasn't Witches' blood but a substance that was just as coveted in Hell. They called it Elixir and it was famous throughout the realm because it contained drops of Witches' blood that had been purified of the poison. It was how Souls got high. As long as it was properly produced, that is. Otherwise they died. It was a risk they were willing to take.

"How do I know it's not Cider?" I asked, narrowing my eyes at Lenora. Cider was pure poison. No creature except a Witch could drink it. Better not to be too trusting.

"Suspicious, are we?"

"I like to be cautious."

"I never would have imagined that about you," she replied with a sardonic smile. She shrugged and tipped the vial over her lips. A droplet fell through the air and she caught it on her tongue, looking at me the whole time. "What do you say now?"

"I think I'll drink it from your lips." I pulled her against me in a long kiss and the Elixir enraptured my mind with its fruity succulence. The Apothecaries were skilled at removing the poison from the blood. One miscalculation and the substance became lethal. Not for those like me, naturally, but Lenora definitely would have died. The three of us drained the vial of its contents and the warm liquid soon took its effect. An intoxicating sensation, especially when combined with the ecstasy of their bodies pressed against mine.

"Can I ask you a question?" Lenora said.

"Sure thing, blondie. Ask me anything you want."

"Who's Stella?"

I froze. I didn't want to think about Stella just then. Anything but. Ever since I'd lost her, I'd done everything I could to avoid thinking of her. Every woman I picked up, every risk I ran was nothing but my desperate attempt to take my mind off Stella.

"Does it seem like the time to bring that up?" Khetra asked her reproachfully.

"She's right. I don't want to think about her right now. She's not important."

"She must be important since you get so upset whenever our mistress takes on her appearance."

I clenched my fists. "She used to be, but she died when I was still back on Earth."

Lenora looked into my eyes. She seemed to want to tell me something. When she finally spoke, my whole world shattered into a million pieces.

"She's out there. In Hell. I've seen her."

I grabbed her by the shoulders, shocked. "What did you just say? It can't be."

"She's out there somewhere," she repeated. "I saw her in Kreeshna's crystal sphere. The mistress has been watching her for a long time now."

My eyes opened wide and I staggered backwards, supporting myself against the wall to avoid falling. It was impossible. I had always believed a Subterranean had helped Stella cross over, had taken her to Eden, where I would never be able to see her again. The thought that I hadn't been able to say goodbye to her had almost destroyed me. How could a creature as pure as she was end up in Hell? "It can't be," I insisted, in a complete daze.

Khetra moved away, annoyed. "Sometimes mortals have dangerous desires, and the Witches know how to fulfill them in exchange for their souls." With this, she smiled. She enjoyed that game.

I didn't.

Stella, in Hell? *She must be terrified.*

My head was awhirl with thoughts, images, terrible conjectures. Before I could overcome my shock, the tower doors suddenly burst open. A Mizhya raced through them in my direction. She had a threatening air, but only a few steps later she arched her back, her eyes opened wide, and she fell facedown on the floor.

I looked up at Faust, who was standing just outside the doors. Lenora and Khetra put themselves on guard, brandishing their weapons. "Stay back, Soldier," the latter ordered him.

He ignored them, urgency in his voice. "Drake, there's something you need to know."

"I already do," I said, nodding, grateful that he had come running to tell me just as soon as he'd found out. Faust knew me well. I'd talked to him several times about Stella when I was too drunk on Elixir to keep my secrets to myself.

"You'd better hurry. Kreeshna is hunting her down."

The blood turned to ice in my veins. I strode over to Faust. "How do you know all this? How?!"

"My Amìsha Anya told me. Kreeshna wants to bring her here and throw her into the Opalion."

I reeled away from Faust, even more devastated than before. Learning that Stella was in Hell had been a shock. Imagining her in the Opalion was too much to bear. So that was why the Witches had been going on Hunts so often recently: they were looking for Stella. She wouldn't last one minute in the Games.

"She'll pit her against you," Khetra broke in, thinking out loud. "She'll want you to kill her in the Opalion to prove your devotion. She'll track her down, no matter what it takes. You can't prevent it."

My eyes widened. This was even worse.

"She's nasty," Lenora said. "It would be just like her."

"Faust, look out!" I shouted.

The Mizhya on the ground had pulled the dagger out of the back of her neck and was poised to attack my friend from behind. Faust blocked the blow and grabbed the weapon. This time he stabbed her beneath the ear—the only spot on the Damned where a dagger thrust was lethal —and the Mizhya exploded in a cloud of dust.

"You killed her!" Lenora cried in dismay.

"She tried to keep me from coming here to warn him," Faust said in his defense.

I barely heard their voices. A deafening thought was pounding in my temples: Stella was out there. "I have to find her before Kreeshna does," I murmured, my heart full of conflicting emotions. Fear . . . and hope. Would I really find Stella again? There was no time for an escape plan. I had to hurry or that hope would also vanish in a cloud of dust.

"Stay where you are," Lenora warned me, guessing my intentions.

Faust blocked her way. "Step aside, unless you want to end up like your friend."

"Try it," the Mizhya shot back, brandishing her dagger, "and the poison on my blade will give you a taste of justice."

Faust attacked Lenora, and Khetra darted toward me. Taking a giant leap, she whipped out a set of double sticks, which I dodged just in time. "Drake, please, don't do anything stupid."

"People tell me that all the time, but I never listen to them," I replied, returning her attack.

"Didn't you say she doesn't matter to you?"

I managed to yank one of the sticks away from her and our weapons slammed together. "I lied. I've spent a lifetime trying to get over losing her, and now that I have a shot at finding her again I'm not going to miss my chance."

Faust dealt a blow to Lenora and she crashed to the ground, out cold. He picked up her dagger and prepared to finish her off, but Khetra stopped him.

"No! Don't kill her." She raised her hands in a gesture of surrender.

"Believe me, I don't want to," Faust said, "but she's going to wake up and tell them everything."

"She won't. You have my word. Don't kill her."

Faust shot me a hesitant glance and when I nodded, he gave them the benefit of the doubt. "All right, but I'll be keeping an eye on her to make sure she doesn't change her mind. The same goes for you."

"I'll make sure it doesn't happen," Khetra promised. She knelt at Lenora's side.

I turned to Faust. "Hey, bud—"

"Don't thank me too much." He cut me off with a cocky smile. "I owed you one after kicking your ass in the Opalion."

"Yeah, right."

He gripped my fist and we man-hugged. "Admit it, it must've been humiliating to be defeated in front of all those people."

I burst out laughing. "Come back and see me when you've gotten all that lymphe out of your bloodstream, then we'll see who kicks whose ass."

Faust laughed. "I'm not giving up such a privilege for you. It was a good fight, though. But you're still just an ex-military player."

"I'll take that as a compliment." I leaned over Lenora and picked up her hooked daggers. "These'll come in handy." I winked at Khetra and she rose to her feet, standing in front of me. We stared at each other for a long moment. I wasn't so sure she wanted to let me go any more. Still, what I saw in her eyes was sadness, not defeat. Finally she stepped aside.

Closing the distance between us, I locked my eyes on hers. "If they find out you let me go, you know what they'll do to you. Can I trust you?"

"I won't betray you. Besides, I have a greater chance of being killed if you stay here."

I nodded, grateful, and brushed my lips against hers. Then I drove the daggers into the rock and leapt over the wall.

"Be careful. It's hell out there," Faust warned me.

"I'll remember that." I mimed a military salute and began to lower myself, but instantly plunged several yards before managing to break my fall. "Whoa!" I exclaimed, planting my feet against the wall and clinging to the daggers. "If I manage to reach the ground in one piece, that is," I said under my breath.

I looked down. *Shit, was I high up!* The twilight made it even more difficult to make out my destination. I shot my head back up to ward off the dizziness. Closing my eyes, I took a deep breath.

Come on, Drake. You got this.

The thought of Stella gave me the drive I needed to snap out of it and continue my descent. I couldn't believe there was actually a chance I might see her again. How on earth had she ended up in Hell?

When I finally reached the ground, I looked around. I hadn't left the Castle even once since I'd gotten there. Large bare trees with twisted branches stood guard outside the fortress, almost like living creatures haunting the grounds. Their tangled roots spread out in every direction. They looked like they were lying in wait for anyone who tried to sneak past, ready to hunt them down. To hunt *me* down. Maybe they really were. I would find out soon enough, because there was no other way to escape from the Castle.

Making my way into the dark wood, I peered around warily. Soon I realized the trees weren't moving, though their trunks looked like faces twisted into grimaces of terror. I laughed to myself. "Shit, Drake. You have one wild imagination."

Something moved behind me and I spun around. A branch was swaying slightly but nothing was there. I shook my head. "Man, I could use a drink." Sheathing Lenora's daggers, I kept walking. I had to get away from there fast, before the Witches came back from the Kryadon. My only hope was that Kreeshna hadn't tracked Stella down yet. How could an innocent, defenseless creature like her be any good at hiding? I didn't dare imagine what Kreeshna would do to her if she found her before I did.

So that was why the Witch continued to take on her appearance. She was testing my loyalty. Stella was still alive and that made her a threat. If Stella's life hadn't been at stake I would have been flattered by Kreeshna's desire for my total devotion. Come to think of it, maybe for the Witch I was only a whim, like everything else. Maybe the fact that my heart had been given to another woman just made the game more exciting to her. I leaned against a boulder as I tried to get my bearings. I had no destination, but I didn't want to end up going back up the road leading to the Castle either.

There was a snort and the rock behind me shoved me away. I spun around, on alert, and watched the rock as it rose up, growing as big as a tank.

"I've got a bad feeling about this," I muttered. Slowly I pulled out the two daggers, prepared to fight. The creature turned, its rocky face inches from mine.

"Holy fuck," I whispered, appalled. In reply, the stone-bear opened its massive jaws and hit me with a savage shriek, its mouth filled with sharp teeth.

If there was one thing I hadn't imagined about Hell, it was that I might be eaten alive by a rock.

3

HELL HAS ITS FAULTS

When the horrible creature stopped screaming at me, I slowly sheathed my knives. "These won't help me any. Unless I decide to tickle you." I hoped it would understand that I wasn't looking for trouble. Living creatures could sense certain things, right?

I backed up. "Okay, now I'm going to slowly leave and let you get back to your nap." The beast spewed a greenish liquid in my direction. "Aw, gross! Hasn't anyone ever taught you manners?"

It shot up, enraged. Another shriek burst from its giant mouth. There were pieces of flesh caught in its teeth. No point hoping it was a vegetarian. It was time to get my ass out of there.

"It's been real!" I bolted off without looking back. "If I survive this I'm going to need a nice, long bath." The animal didn't seem to be following me, but just to be on the safe side I didn't stop. I didn't want to be digested by a big rock with fangs.

I spotted the mouth of a cave and slipped inside to catch my breath. In there I would be safe from that creature and from the Witches, who must have returned from the Hunt by now. What if Kreeshna had already noticed I was gone? How long did I have before she came looking for me?

A dim glow caught my eye. It was the only shaft of light in the darkness of the cave. I followed it to an open space barely illuminated by a hole in the ceiling that led outside. There was something hidden there in the shadows. I tried to move cautiously. It looked like a human shape but there was no telling for sure. When I was close enough I realized I was right.

It was a girl.

It took me a moment to get over my shock. Maybe I had gotten there too late.

Her arms were stretched out and her wrists were chained to opposite walls of the cave. Her hair hung down, blocking my view of her face, but she was clearly a teenager.

I moved closer. She wore a white dress splattered with dark patches, the blood of the Damned. The largest patch was in the center, where a long piece of wood protruded from her abdomen. "My God, what did they do to you?" I gulped. It was a gruesome sight. The girl moved her dangling head and I almost jumped out of my skin.

"Hey, you awake?" Without thinking twice, I took hold of the wooden stick buried in her flesh and pulled it out. She inhaled noisily, as though she hadn't had air in days. "Who did this to you?"

She raised her dark, weary eyes to me, but they instantly shot to something behind me and filled with terror. I spun around, the stick still in my hand, and froze. Skeletal men had crawled in through the hole in the ceiling and were creeping down the walls like giant spiders. I must have ended up in their nest and the girl was their meal.

"Stop right there!" I ordered them, backing toward her protectively. The cave filled with the grunts of the creatures, who continued to creep down the walls. To my amazement, one of them spoke in a raspy voice: "It is not wise to defend the Unholy."

"I've met Unholy creatures and this girl is definitely not one of them," I blurted. But then I noticed that the girl behind me was sniffing me. I turned around, horrified. Her eyes had become two dark pools, her gaze possessed, and her teeth those of a shark, smeared with black blood. "Holy fuck!" I shot away from her and all the creatures leapt to the ground, trapping me. "Okay, my bad."

I had to pay more attention in my attempts to identify the Damned. As for the intentions of the shady characters surrounding me, I had no doubt: it was not good news. "What do you say I slink off and leave you guys to your disgusting dinner?" I looked around for a way out, but there wasn't one.

"You will go nowhere." They emitted a strange noise again, one that sounded like the hissing of an angry cat.

"You are both our prey. Two is better than one. There are many of us. We must eat," one of the more sociable ones explained, almost like it wanted to convince me.

My grip tightened on the stick. "Sorry. I'm not on the

menu today." I spun the weapon around and struck the scrawny Soul full in the face. It was pretty easy to send it sprawling on the ground, as light as it was. Standing over it, I drove the stick into its skull. "Though I'm sure I taste delicious."

"Uh-oh." The smile died on my lips when another skeleton crept out of the shadows and confronted me, angrier than ever. It let out a shrill shriek that echoed through the cave and the entire swarm rushed at me. "Okay, bring it, you bags of bones!" I struck left, right, and center without a second's pause. I knew that if I stopped they would overpower me. I was outnumbered but had no intention of dying, knowing that Stella was out there, alone and defenseless. I had to find her and protect her.

One of the creatures jumped on me and knocked me to the ground at the Unholy girl's feet. I struggled, trying to shake it off. It was snapping its teeth rapidly, hoping to bite into my face. Touching it was horrific. "Man, you're disgusting." Taut skin covered its skeleton and its black eyes were sunk deep in their orbits. "Now I get why you want to eat me." I shoved it away and heard its bones snapping.

Standing right behind me, the Unholy girl writhed in her chains, drawing my attention. From my position all I could see was up her skirt. I covered my eyes with my hand. "Beg your pardon, miss."

I shot to my feet. This time I was the one to attack. I advanced to the center of the cave and took them on one by one, determined to annihilate them all.

Suddenly they all stopped.

"What is it? Tired already? I can keep going all day long. Come on, bring it!"

The skeletons didn't move. Another creature emerged from the darkness. It was like them, but bigger. Something was showing beneath its skin. I squinted and was left sickened. It was the shape of an entire creature it had devoured. "Man, are you nasty."

With a bound, it pounced on me. It was far heavier than the others—it must have been their leader—and I struggled to keep it away. It bit my shoulder and I cried out in pain. Hearing my cry, all the creatures in the cave let out a squeal of delight and rushed at me. I knew I was done for. My immortality would be fucked if they ate me. Christ, what a shitty end I had in store for me.

A sudden burst of light lit up our surroundings. I thought it was the light at the end of the tunnel people always talked about, but all at once the creatures withdrew, focusing on their new objective. I propped myself up on my elbows, dazed, and squinted to see better. Tongues of fire danced around the cave, forcing the skeletons into a corner. Their shrill cries pierced my ears.

"Gurdan, I'll hold them back. Get the girl."

The world stood still when I heard that voice. I turned to look at her and our eyes locked for a long moment. A black tattoo concealed her face, but I would have known those eyes anywhere. There was no doubt it was her.

"Stella," I murmured. I couldn't believe she was really there. She didn't look like the defenseless girl I remembered. She was strong, a brand-new creature forged by Hell. A bow in her hand, she was dressed like a warrior, her voice authoritative, commanding.

I lost myself in her eyes. All along I'd been afraid I wouldn't find her and instead, she was the one who had ended up finding me. She'd even come to my rescue.

Her gaze suddenly went hard. She nocked an arrow and shot it straight at me. Cringing, I looked down, staring at the weapon sticking out of my chest. I looked back up at Stella, shocked.

She hurled a rope out of the cave and vanished a second later as I thudded to the ground.

4

THE PRICE OF SURVIVAL

I groaned, slowly regaining consciousness. The arrow Stella had shot me with must have been poisoned. The memory of what had happened hit me like a punch in the gut. Then I remembered the hole left by the arrow. That must have been what hurt so much.

Had I really found Stella? And why had she tried to kill me? She must have known I was a Subterranean and that I wouldn't actually die. Or hadn't she?

I opened my eyes and found myself bound like a sausage with my back against a tree. When I squirmed to break free the ropes dug into my wounds and I had to stop, gritting my teeth from the sharp pain. Before me lay a dark forest, but I could hear a fire crackling behind me. "Hey! Anybody there?"

"Prisoner awake," a deep male voice grunted.

"Prisoner?" I said, bewildered. "There must be some mistake. I'm the guy who needed to be saved."

"Maybe hungry, him. We give food?" the same man asked, but no one answered. I heard someone come up to me with heavy footsteps. The swift stroke of an ax shook the tree I was tied to and the ropes went slack.

"Finally!" I exclaimed. I turned around to look the person in the eye, but banged into the chest of a giant as big as a tank. He held an enormous ax in his fist. I raised my hands in surrender. That was one lethal weapon.

The second he stepped aside I saw her. The sight took my breath away. Stella was sitting beside a fire, looking down at her meal. The man grabbed my hands and bound them together.

"Hey!" I protested. In silence he pushed me toward the fire. "Wait, you don't mean to eat *me*, do you?!" I exclaimed, worried. He shoved me down, forcing me to sit, then plunked a bowl of meat on my knee. Stella was on the opposite side of the fire. "What's going on? Stella, it's me! Don't you recognize me?" I said.

She muttered something and finally looked up. The look in her eye was cold, distant, nothing like the Stella I used to know. "Never call me that again," she warned me sternly.

My eyes widened. I couldn't believe those were her first words to me. "What are you talking about? You're Stella, *my* Stella. We were together, on Earth. What's happened to you?"

"I'm Kahlena and Hell is my home."

I froze. Had she forgotten me? Forgotten us? "Is this what Hell's done to you? What have you become?"

She stood up, grabbed her bow and quiver, and disappeared into the forest without deigning to look at me. I ran my bound hands over my face, anguished. She was so different from the person I'd once known. Now she seemed like an Amazon in those dark leather pants and armed to the teeth. She wore fingerless gloves and around her waist was an arsenal of weapons. Stella had always had a brave spirit, but on Earth she'd shown it by helping others, not by going around shooting arrows into them.

"Meal," Gurdan grunted, pointing at the bowl of meat before me. He was a big, burly man with a funny patch of curly hair above his ears. The rest of his head was bald. He looked like an ogre, he was so intent on devouring his ration of meat.

I picked up my bowl and nodded my thanks to him. At least it smelled delicious.

Stella reappeared through the bushes and sat down again across from me. I had always adored her exotic charm, and her golden complexion glowed like never before in the firelight. Back in the skeletons' den, in the dimness of the twilight, it had looked like half her head was shaved. Instead, her hair was woven into an intricate braid close to her scalp that left the right side of her face uncovered. I studied her tattoo: it was a mask of black ink that framed her eyes and made its way down her cheeks, accentuating her sharp features.

"Stop staring at me and eat," she snapped without looking at me.

I couldn't believe I'd found Stella and that she'd become so cold and detached. "I still can't get over it. You shot me in the chest with an arrow," I said, brimming with resentment. "You could've killed me." If I couldn't elicit in her the same emotions I was feeling, maybe I could at least manage to make her react. Her emotions couldn't have disappeared completely.

She said nothing and continued to eat.

"Why'd you bring me here if you don't know who I am any more? You might as well have left me in the cave with those skeletons," I said sharply. Still she said nothing. I was angry and frustrated; she'd killed my joy at finding her again with one of her arrows, just as she'd almost taken my life. I grumbled, touching my chest. This seemed to draw her attention. She looked at me for a minute, then went back to her meal.

"You know what? I'm just going to shut up and eat my food too—whatever it is." My hands bound, I bit into a piece of the meat and found it wasn't too bad. "At least it tastes good," I murmured, still eating. "So Gurdan, where's the girl? You got her out of there too, didn't you?"

"Girl," he repeated, his voice gruff. "Eat."

"Okay, okay," I said, singsong, frowning. "You must have a screw loose," I muttered to myself.

"Girl! Eat!" he bellowed, banging his fist on the ground. Was he offended?

"Hey, hey! Don't get all bent out of shape." I turned to Stella, who was hiding a smile. It almost took my breath away. It was so nice to see her smile again. "What's gotten into your friend, anyway? What's he saying?"

"Gurdan was answering your question, that's all."

I looked around. "Well, where's the girl, then? You got her tied up someplace?"

"She's right in front of you," she said, sneering.

I felt a wave of nausea when I understood: we were eating her. *I* was eating her. I gagged and spat, revolted.

"What's wrong? Didn't you say it tasted good?"

"Sure, before I knew I'd met her!"

"Ooh, what a princess," Stella said mockingly. She had become heartless. That must have been how she'd managed to survive. She nodded at Gurdan, who stood up and walked away.

We stared at the fire for a long time. It was Stella who broke the silence. "How long have you been here?"

"I'm not sure exactly, but I've been in the Castle the whole time."

She shot to her feet, on guard, her weapon pointed at me. "At the Castle? You're one of them?"

"Calm down. I'm not an ally of the Witches—though I pretended I was."

"Why are you here? And how did you escape?"

"Some friends helped me out. When I heard you were still alive, that you were out here somewhere, I came running. I had to find you before the Witches did."

Her face grew dark. "I'm not alive."

"You are for me," I blurted.

"Not like you remember. You've seen what we're forced to do here. And this is nothing."

I stared at the remains of the girl we had been feasting on. Stella was one of the Damned, but to me it made no difference. She had been forced to adapt. She was still my Stella and I would find a way to make her remember.

"At least you didn't eat *me*," I joked, to break the tension.

"Not yet." Stella laughed and I did too, poorly concealing how worried I was. The ogre didn't make me feel very safe, big as he was. A deep silence fell between us and she glanced at me. "I've dreamed about them."

"About who?" I frowned. It was clear who she meant, but I asked anyway.

"About the Witches. About *you*."

My eyes widened. She had dreamed about me. I wanted to know more about her dream but Gurdan came back and tossed something at my feet.

"For Princess."

Stella laughed and I cast her a sidelong glance. "Not funny." I picked the animal up by its hind legs, trying to figure out what it was. It looked like a squirrel with the snout of a porcupine. "You're not expecting me to eat this raw, are you?"

"Naturally. We're the Insane. We eat our meat raw." She stared at me, her expression suddenly evil as the tension around us grew. The Insane were the worst Souls among all the Damned, the ones who had lost every last trace of their humanity. I had faced lots of them when battling in the Opalion and fuck, were they vicious.

Stella burst out laughing. "Don't worry, I'm not a freaking zombie. Not yet." She threw her dagger hard and the animal flew from my hands and onto the embers of the fire. "You can always cook it."

I lowered my hand, stunned. "Perfect aim. Remind me never to argue with you."

"Kahlena friend Gurdan. Princess fight Kahlena, I kill Princess." The ogre bit into a chunk of meat, staring at me menacingly.

"I was kidding, pal. Try to relax."

Stella smiled to herself and began to speak in a strange language. To my surprise, Gurdan answered in the same tongue. He seemed to have a good command of it, while I didn't understand a word. The giant stood up and went to lean against the tree trunk.

"Just because you don't know a language doesn't mean you're stupid," Stella said once we were alone.

"Thank you. Finally, a compliment."

"I wasn't talking about you. Gurdan knows Grimtholk really well, but he's been here so long he's forgotten our language. I'm teaching it to him again."

"Oh." So maybe Gurdan wasn't as stupid as he seemed. "And Grimtholk would be . . . ?"

"The common language of the Souls in Hell." Stella lay down on a pile of pelts and turned her back to me. "Get some sleep now."

"What, you mean he's going to stay there watching us the whole time?"

"He doesn't sleep much. He'll take a turn standing guard."

"And who's going to guard me from him?" I shot back sarcastically.

"There are more important things for you to worry about. Like taking a bath. You stink worse than a Molock."

After a few sniffs I realized she was right. The greenish liquid had dried on me and you could probably smell its stench from a mile away. The worst smell wasn't coming from me, though, but from my wounds. The skeleton's bite itched and the hole in my chest from Stella's arrow still stung. Not to mention the ho le it had left in my heart.

I shrugged. Bathing was the last thing on my mind. Instead, I sat there staring at Stella, lying just steps away from me. Not even in my dreams had I ever imagined I would see her again. Now she was so close, yet I had never felt so far away from her. I wished I could lie down beside her and hold her tight, inhale her scent, lose myself in the warmth of her body. Instead, I hadn't even been able to hug her. And it hurt.

I turned the dog tag I always wore over in my fingers. I never should have volunteered for the war. I had left her alone, promising I would come back. Instead, I had lost her. That memento was supposed to have been for her, but when I returned to give it to her it was too late. She was gone.

I picked up a pelt, spread it out on the ground, and lay down at her side. Maybe I couldn't embrace her, but at least she was there with me again. I looked at her, captivated by her face, and knew I could never let her go again.

I didn't care how long it took me. I was going to win her back.

5

HELL IS INSIDE ME

The massive door opened in front of us, revealing an enormous hall surrounded by towering windows. Black reigned everywhere in the Castle. Even the floor was a slab of shiny black stone, like a diamond of death. The only color that broke the darkness was a red patch at the foot of the large throne, the symbol of the Witches: a semi-circle with an upside-down V and panther claw marks. The same symbol was carved into the center of the Arena. Whatever form the battlefield assumed, that symbol was always there, reminding me who was in charge.

The two Witches pushed me forward and a swarm of black butterflies fluttered around me, agitated. The iron cords binding my wrists burned my skin with every step, as did the lash marks on my back. The Witches had been pretty clear about how things went for prisoners. I had seen it with my own two eyes down in the torture chambers that were filled with the screams of the Subterraneans they had imprisoned. I had even had a taste of it on my own skin. But not all of the Subterraneans in the Castle were down in the prisons. I'd seen lots of them walking freely among the Witches, almost as though we hadn't been two enemy races since time immemorial. At first the thought seemed crazy to me, but then I'd seen the mark of the Children of Eve on their left arms, just like mine. There was no doubt about it: they were Subterraneans.

The Witches stopped and I looked up at the throne, black butterflies carved into it. Before me was Sophìa, queen of the Underworld. She stared at me in silence with her lapis lazuli eyes. Blind rage simmered within me, but she wasn't the one causing it. I clenched my fists when Kreeshna rose from the chair to her left. She was the Witch who had tried to steal my soul, tormenting me for decades in an attempt to subjugate me and make me serve her in Hell.

"In the end you've come to me," she said mockingly, drawing closer with graceful steps. Her smug expression made the blood boil in my veins. She stopped a step away from my face, her black eyes probing mine. The serpent inside her broke through her skin and slithered out. She seemed to enjoy the sensation. The sight was at once spine-chilling and sensual. She leaned over me and her lips touched my ear in a whisper. "You and my Dakor will have a lot of time to get to know one another here at the Castle." The serpent hissed, coiling around her neck. He too, like his mistress, seemed excited by the idea. "On your knees, Child of Eve." Behind me, the redheaded Witch who had escorted me there cracked her whip.

I hesitated, returning Kreeshna's challenging look. Then I did as she said, glaring at her the whole time.

"Soldier Drake Reeves," she proclaimed solemnly, "do you resist or do you submit?" In the grim silence, Kreeshna's Dakor hissed again. The Witch smiled, reading the answer in my mind.

"I submit."

The Dakor lunged toward me and sank its poisonous fangs into my neck. The venom burned in my veins. Or maybe what hurt so much was my anger at being forced to make that choice.

"Sweet dreams, sugarplum," Kreeshna murmured.

Her image went blurry and I crumpled to the floor.

I WOKE WITH A START, my breathing ragged and my fists clenched. The sight of Kreeshna with that fucking Dakor had left my nerves aflame. Trying to calm my anger, I ran a hand down my face. I'd never dreamed when I was on Earth. Another bizarre effect of being in Hell. It hadn't been just a dream, though. It was a memory, a memory of the pact of subjugation I had made with the Witches. At the time it had seemed like the most advantageous thing to do, but the more I thought about the power Kreeshna had wielded over me day by day, the more my hatred grew.

I turned toward Stella, but she was gone.

Her things were still there, so she couldn't have gone far. Worried, I sat up, a groan of pain escaping me. The wound on my shoulder hurt like hell. Gurdan was still sitting at the foot of the tree, his mouth open and his breathing heavy. He had nodded off.

"Great guard dog," I mumbled, passing him. He grabbed my ankle in a powerful grip that almost made me cry out, but then his hand fell heavily to the ground. He was still sleeping. "Ouch!" I muttered, slipping away.

The sound of lapping water came from a distance. There must be a river somewhere around there. I still stank.

Maybe it was time to take Stella's advice and clean up. I crossed a thicket and found myself on the shore of a lake.

"Finally, a little luck."

It didn't take me long to get undressed, since I wore only the standard brown pants the Witches gave all their minions. I had never seen a single Subterranean wearing a shirt in the Castle. They seemed to be forbidden there. Sometimes they even had us do battle barefoot.

Despite the cold, I waded into the water. When I dove in I felt the grime slide off me. The cold stung my still-open wounds. I closed my eyes, driving off the images that rushed through my mind: the Arena, blood, and then Stella's eyes, black and brilliant. I was captivated by the energy they emanated.

I would have stayed there for hours but I didn't want her to get back to the camp and not find me there. I rinsed my hair and tied it up tight on top of my head as I waded back to shore. Stella was there, crouched on a branch, her bowstring drawn, an arrow aimed at me.

Slowly, I raised my hands in surrender. "You don't mean to skewer me again, I hope."

She lowered her weapon, still staring at me as I came out of the water, naked and dripping wet. I didn't dare hope it was desire I saw in her eyes. "Want me to get you a soda and some popcorn?"

Stella tossed me my clothes and walked off, as always with a grim look on her face. Definitely not desire. I pulled my pants on and went back to the camp. She was already there, sitting on her pile of pelts. She had put away her weapon, so she didn't mean to kill me. But then why had she aimed an arrow at me at the lake? I clenched my jaw. She didn't trust me. Or maybe she didn't trust herself?

Pointing to a spot near her, I asked, "Can I sit down there or will I be risking my life?" When she didn't answer I hesitated, but finally she nodded and I went over to her. "You always so quiet?"

"Unlike you," she shot back without looking at me. On her lap was a pile of strange leaves that she was skillfully weaving together. "Come closer," she suddenly told me.

"It's about time!" I leaned in to kiss her, but she whipped out a knife as swiftly as a panther and pointed it at my throat. "Okay, I misunderstood. No need to get so worked up."

She lowered her eyes and rested the knife on the ground. "Sorry," she murmured, surprising me.

"No problem," I said, momentarily startled into seriousness. I wasn't sure she had always been so brooding. She seemed torn. Stella was no longer the person I'd once known. She had become something else, something I would have to learn to know. And yet, beneath that mask of ink, my Stella was still there, I was sure of it. Whatever was troubling her, I was there with her now and I wasn't going to leave her again.

This time it was she who leaned toward me. I stared at her as she daubed my wound with a white paste. I gritted my teeth against the searing pain.

"The wound is infected. This should make it heal quickly. It's an antiseptic."

"You made it yourself?" I asked her, impressed. She nodded, her expression modest. "I was afraid you were in danger out here, but I see you really know how to take care of yourself."

"In Hell you either learn to survive or you die."

"Yeah, I'd figured that out," I grunted, examining the wound she was medicating. The bite marks were deep and they'd turned from red to a yellowish brown. "What were those creatures, anyway?" I still couldn't shake the thought of the taut, slimy skin covering their bones.

"They were Gluttons."

"Ya think?" I shot back, getting a smile out of her.

"Hell follows certain rules. Whatever it was you most desired on Earth might end up being your punishment here. The Gluttons are those who during their lifetimes acted unscrupulously not only to get what they wanted but to get more of it . . . and more, and more, leaving innocent souls to pay the price for their choices. Their insatiable hunger for money, power, or whatever else it was turned them into ravenous souls tormented by a longing that can never be satiated. Not even the most delicious feasts can satisfy them now. They get hungrier and hungrier, and that makes them weak. You were lucky. You could've run into far more dangerous creatures."

"Hey, those guys were pretty hungry and I bet I looked delicious. They were totally dangerous," I assured her. I had battled far more ferocious creatures in the Opalion, but those skeletons had given me a run for my money.

"You'll change your mind," Stella said flatly, bandaging the bite with the damp green leaves she had braided. She moved on to the wound on my chest and silence fell between us. "Sorry about this."

"Two apologies, one after the other? This is my lucky day."

"You never take anything seriously, do you?"

"Well, my girlfriend did try to kill me, so sorry if cracking a joke helps me cope."

"I'm not your girlfriend," she pointed out.

I clasped my hand over hers, against my chest. Her fingers reacted, touching mine. "I don't agree with you there either."

"That's your problem." She pulled her hand away and glared at me. I stared back at her, intense and brazenly close. I couldn't hold back a little smile as I probed her eyes with mine until she was forced to turn away. I had spent years grieving for her and now that I had found her again I had no intention of letting her get away. Sooner or later I would wear down her defenses.

Stella went back to treating my wounds.

"Do you trust him?" I jutted my chin toward Gurdan.

"He's okay, but don't go around striking up friendships. In Hell, Souls are driven by two things: the survival instinct or a thirst for blood. All you can hope for are fleeting alliances. No one trusts anyone else. You'd be better off doing the same."

"I've had a taste of it." I touched the wound she herself had inflicted on me. "You treated it for me, though, and that's a step in the right direction."

"Only because your red blood would attract too many predators. Subterraneans are a precious commodity down here."

"You could've left me there, but you didn't. You didn't run off."

"For the same reason. Like I said, Subterraneans are a precious commodity."

"Is that what you are? A mercenary?"

"You're clearly a guy who asks a lot of questions."

"And you're clearly good at dodging them."

"I didn't really mean to kill you, if that's what you want to know."

"Lucky me, then. If it's true, that is."

Losing her temper, she tugged on my woven bandages and tied them tightly in place. "I'm not a liar. I saw the mark on your arm. You're a Soldier of Eve. You can't die. Not from an arrow, at least."

I looked steadily into her eyes. "That doesn't mean it doesn't hurt like hell."

"I've already said I'm sorry."

"An arrow square in the chest deserves more than a simple 'I'm sorry,' don't you think?"

"Shh!" Stella shot to her feet, holding up a finger to silence me.

"No, I mean it. If you really want me to forgive you, that would take at least a ki—"

Behind me, Stella clapped her hand over my mouth. "Would you shut up? Someone's out there," she whispered, on her guard. She gestured for me to get up and then woke Gurdan, also covering his mouth with her hand. There were noises around us. We had no way of knowing what was lurking in the Copse.

"Stay behind me," I whispered to her, stepping out in front.

She pulled two long staffs from the quiver on her back and walked out ahead of me. "This is no time to kid around."

"I wasn't kidding around. Now that I'm here, I mean to protect you."

"I don't need to be protected."

"Really? You want to argue now, of all times?!"

Another step and we found them straight ahead of us: a flock of huge birds with long, sharp beaks, as tall as humans. They weren't there for us; they were busy nosing around on the ground in search of something.

"They haven't seen us," I whispered to Stella. "Maybe we can slip away without them noticing."

"Good idea," she whispered. "There are too many of them."

I counted at least eight. One let out a strange call and we cringed.

"What is that thing, a seal dressed up in feathers?"

"Shut up and keep walking."

The animal went back to scouring the ground. No, not the ground, I was disgusted to realize, but its prey. It was feeding. On what, I wasn't sure, given the shadowy twilight.

"It looks hungry. I hope that's a big branch covered with fruit. What do they normally eat?" I asked.

The raptor tossed something into the air and skewered it on its long beak as it continued to writhe. It was a human Soul.

Gurdan stepped on something that snapped. We froze in

our tracks. One of the raptors howled again and shot its head in our direction. It had spotted us.

"They eat *us*! Run!" Stella shouted, sprinting away.

"I shouldn't have asked."

The raptors were incredibly fast and chased after us like we were juicy rare steaks. Their black beaks were like hollow tubes through which they sucked their victims' blood.

"We've got to split up!" Stella said, still running.

"Forget it. I'm not leaving you."

"It wasn't a suggestion." Stella whipped out her bow and shot an arrow upward. She grabbed the end of the long cord tied to the arrowhead and swung herself up to a branch high above, disappearing among the foliage. A shrill whistle filled the treetops and all at once the raptors followed it, digging their beaks into the tree trunks to climb them.

"Stella!" I shouted, but there was no reply. "Fuck!" I couldn't stand the thought of losing her again, but I couldn't risk stopping. I looked back over my shoulder. Two of the bloodsuckers were still chasing me. "I bet you're females." The creatures' only reply was to let out that weird howl again. I shook my head over how ugly they were. One of them sped up and rushed out in front of me, forcing me to come to a halt.

I was trapped.

An even more bizarre gurgle rose from their throats. I hoped it wasn't a call to draw the rest of the flock. Now that they were so close I could see them better. The noise they were making was coming from flaps in their necks. Their eyes, to the sides of their beaks, were two bulging balls that darted around, pointing at their prey. Except for the red tuft atop their heads, their feathers were gray. They had long, swift legs and a slender tail that stuck out stiffly. Or maybe they were just happy to see me.

"Even with all the monsters I've faced in the Opalion, you guys are definitely the ugliest creatures I've ever seen." The difference was that during the Games the worst-case scenario was that I was killed and taken to the regeneration pools. Out here I risked being disemboweled.

Seeming to understand my insult, the raptors attacked. When I dove to the ground and rolled away to escape their razor-sharp beaks, they crashed into each other, making me laugh. "You're not only ugly, you're stupid too." The beasts howled and one of them charged me, enraged. "C'mon, bring it." I waited until it was close, grabbed its neck and leapt onto its back. I had ridden an ostrich once. It wasn't so different.

Under my weight the animal went wild, thrashing around as it tried to throw me to the ground. I clung to its head but accidentally touched its beak, cutting my hand. "Shit, is that sharp!"

The smell of my red blood sent them both into a frenzy. The other raptor attacked its companion, wanting to steal its prey. I tried to guide it away from the blows, clinging to its short, bristly feathers. Their beaks clashed together like swords. It looked like a fencing match between two birds. Black blood spurted every which way. They were prepared to kill each other just to have me, and I instantly realized it wasn't such a bad idea.

"There's something I learned from the Games." I grabbed the bird's beak and the moment the other one charged us again I drove it into its skull. It froze and toppled to the ground. "When you don't have a weapon, invent one." The animal beneath me bucked, trying yet again to throw me off its back.

"Having fun?" Stella reappeared atop a tree, her arms crossed and her expression amused. *Man, was I happy to see her again.*

"Want to go for a spin, gorgeous?" I wielded my finest smile, but the beast threw me off-balance and I almost ended up on the ground. "Hey, don't make me look bad," I said reproachfully before turning back to Stella. "C'mon, I'll give you a ride. Why carry your dinner around when dinner can carry you?"

"Because sooner or later *you* might end up being dinner. Here." Stella took a dagger out of a sheath strapped to her thigh and tossed it to me. I caught it, but this time I really did lose my balance and fell off. All I saw a second later was the raptor's beak plunging straight down at me. I rolled away, barely dodging it, grabbed the beast while its beak was still stuck in the ground, and plunged my knife into its throat. The raptor whimpered and flopped to the ground. I raised my eyes to Stella, who grabbed a vine and swung down.

She nodded with approval. "Nice work."

"What happened to yours?"

"I shook them off," she said. "It wasn't my first time. They're stupid animals. And they aren't the only ones, it seems." She grabbed my hand roughly and examined it. "You can't hold a sword by the blade and expect not to get cut," she said, frowning.

"I knew I'd get cut."

"Well, then, you're crazy as well as stupid."

"A little." I winked at her.

Scowling, she pulled out another one of her damp leaf bandages and wound it around my hand. It must have been made of seaweed.

I stared at her, fascinated by her face. Lost in thought, she touched my blood, as she had with the wound on my chest. Who knew what she was thinking? My blood was red, not black like the other Souls' in Hell. Not like hers. Stella, too, was one of the Damned. Maybe my blood was reminding her of what she'd become, of what she'd lost.

Reaching over, I tucked a lock of her hair behind her ear, my fingers lingering on her skin. She seemed to tilt her head slightly toward my hand. Or maybe I'd just imagined it. It hurt to have her so near and yet so far away. I wished I could hold her close and take her away from there.

"Let's get moving. We're too exposed here." She walked off, leaving me with my hand in midair. I lowered it to my side, balling it into a fist to keep myself from punching something.

Bending over one of the raptors, she took out her dagger.

"What are you doing?"

"What do you think? Stockpiling weapons."

I went to her side. She had chopped off the animal's beak and was cleaning it, scraping off the flesh still sticking to it. "You going to stand there watching me or do you want to help?"

"I'd rather do it my way." I grabbed the beak of the second raptor and tore it off with my bare hands.

She stared at me, surprised by my strength. "You made its brain splatter out. Now you'll have to clean it off."

Well, it wasn't like I'd expected her to sing my praises. "Yes, ma'am," I replied sarcastically. I handed her the knife she'd tossed me.

"Come on, hurry up."

"Are we going someplace in particular?"

"Someplace your sharp tongue won't get us hacked to bits."

I shrugged. "Sounds like a plan."

Once they were clean, we packed up our new weapons and resumed walking. Stella was right. We were an easy target for beasts lying in wait. Especially when carrying the raptors. We had to find a place to hide.

"What happened to your friend Gurdan?"

"He'll know how to find me if he wants to."

"You sure they didn't kill him?"

"He knows how to take care of himself. Besides, that's a risk we all run down here."

Her reply irritated me. Did she really not care about anybody? Would she not even care at all about me? "When did you get to be so bitchy?"

"Personal bonds are only for mortal souls. Not for us, the Damned."

I grabbed her arm to stop her and looked her in the eye. Her expression was stony. "The Stella I used to know would never have said that."

"I told you, I'm Kahlena. The person you used to know is gone."

"You can't really believe that."

"If you can't accept it, that's your problem," she said, as cold and aggressive as ever.

I couldn't stand the distance she was putting between us. The closer I got, the farther away she went. "Let me tell you, the new you is a real bitch."

"What would you know?" She jerked her arm free and shoved me in the chest, suddenly furious. "You're a Subterranean. You can't die." She shoved me again and I let her do it, let her vent. "Everything's one big joke to you and why not? You know you'll wake up again no matter what. For me, this is a world of blood and ash!" Another rough shove and I grabbed her by the wrists. Her eyes blazed with rage, but what I saw in them was a different emotion. Her coldness was only a shield. I struggled to keep myself from pulling her to me because I knew if I did she would close herself off again. If she was going to open up to me, I needed her to keep going. Only then would I find my way in.

"Do you have any idea how much I've suffered? What I've been through since I've been here? You don't know what Hell really is. Survival has its price. There's no room for personal bonds." Her voice was brimming with tension.

"You're wrong. I know perfectly well what hell is. I've known it since I lost you. For me, there could never be a worse hell."

"*You* left *me*!" she screamed.

Her answer turned me to stone. "You—you remember?"

Stella stared at me and in her eyes I saw the storm raging within her. She turned her back to keep me from reading any further. A knot gripped my stomach. Stella *remembered?*

"I didn't leave you," I said, frustrated. "I went away to war."

"What's the difference?" she hissed, turning to face me.

"I was coming back."

"You didn't."

"Yes I did." I stepped toward her, closing the distance between us. "I requested a furlough and went home to you, but you were gone."

"Because I was a stupid, foolish little girl. I left my family, my home, to join you. I enlisted in the Red Cross, but I was sent to Normandy. They parachuted us onto the field along with so many soldiers, but my group and I never even made it to the ground. They machine-gunned us during our descent."

"That's horrible," I murmured. I knew the story, but hearing it from her lips was heartbreaking.

"*Horrible* doesn't even begin to describe what I've been through. And it's all your fault," she said, her voice full of resentment.

So that was why Stella hated me so much: she blamed me for her having ended up here. That whole time I had assumed that when Stella died, a Subterranean had helped her soul cross over, accompanying her to Eden. Now I could imagine why that hadn't happened. A Witch must have convinced her to follow her in exchange for making Stella's greatest wish come true.

"It was me . . . I was your wish."

She snorted. "At least the Witch ended up keeping her promise. Sometimes wishes are granted to us when we don't want them any more."

Her words hurt, but I couldn't blame her. "I'm sorry," I murmured, devastated. "I never would have wanted you to go through all this because of me."

"Your apologizing can't change the way things are."

I stopped her again. "I'm here now."

She looked down at my hand on her arm and raised her eyes to mine. "It's too late."

I swallowed. Deep in my chest I had the terrible feeling I'd lost her forever. I'd thought Hell had erased me from her heart, but this was even worse. Stella remembered, but it wasn't enough to bring her back to me. Just the opposite, in fact. She hated me for what I had done to her. It wasn't just a question of winning her back. I had to make amends.

"It's not too late. I'll get you out of this living hell."

"If you really believe that, you're delusional." She turned her back on me, resignation in her voice. "No one can get out of Hell. You can only hope to survive."

I watched her as she walked away. No. I wouldn't give up so easily. I would keep my promise and bring her back.

The ground trembled beneath our feet, as though in protest. Stella turned to me, her troubled eyes locked on mine. The next second, Hell burst open, swallowing her up.

6

TO EACH HIS OWN HELL

"Stella!" I shouted, rushing to the chasm that had opened in the earth.

An arrow shot out of the darkness of the abyss and I dodged it just in time. A cord was tied to one end of it but the arrow missed its target, stopped in midair, and began to fall back down.

Without thinking twice I leapt over the chasm to grab it. "Got it!" I came to a rolling halt on the other side, but Stella's weight dragged me back toward the edge. "Stellaaa!"

"I'm here!" she shouted. Stella was shrouded in darkness but her voice was loud and clear. I had to hang on to her.

The cord slipped again. She was trying to climb up it, but it was making my grip unstable. "Don't move," I shouted, hoping she would listen to me for once. "I'll pull you up." I planted my feet firmly on the ground and wound the rope around my palm. Clenching my jaw, I endured the pain: the wound inflicted by the raptor still burned. Stella was right, it wasn't wise to intentionally get hurt in Hell. Still, I had experienced worse.

I gritted my teeth, my muscles taut from the strain. With one last savage grunt of effort I pulled her up over the edge. Our eyes lingered on each other as I held her tight.

"Hi," I whispered, my breathing ragged. She smiled, but Hell trembled again and we shot to our feet. "What's going on?" I asked, uneasy. It felt like the entire kingdom was about to erupt.

"We're near the volcano. We need to get out of here!" A burst of air announced the eruption of a geyser, just steps away from us. "This way, quick!"

I followed Stella through what looked like a twisted forest of giant boulders that spread out before us. It wasn't easy to dodge the geysers that sprang up with no warning and threatened to burn us. When the heat became suffocating, I looked up and saw it: a huge volcano with crystal-clear lava. What was coming out of its crater wasn't fire. Hell spewed poison instead, disintegrating everything in its path. I scrambled onto a boulder that was sheltered from its spray.

"This way!" I shouted to Stella, who ran toward me as the geysers erupted more and more ferociously. Once more I heard a growl rise from the depths of Hell: its grim warning before the ground burst open again. My eyes bulged when I saw that the fissure was streaking toward Stella.

"Take my hand!" I called urgently, leaning over the rock. Stella looked behind her and gaped as the entire world split in two. She wasn't going to make it.

"Come on, run!" She took a giant leap and threw

herself into the void. Her hand grabbed mine and I gripped it tightly. Beneath her, a river of poison flowed. One of the raptors we had brought with us slid down and was vaporized in midair. We stared at each other, panting, our eyes full of fear. It was the first time I had seen her so vulnerable.

"I was really afraid I was going to lose you," I blurted.

She clung to the rock and pulled herself up. "Get used to the feeling, soldier," she said, putting up her defenses again.

"I just saved you. You could at least say thanks."

"I would've managed on my own. I don't need you," she flung back harshly over her shoulder as she strode out of the stone labyrinth to a spot where the ground was more stable.

Inside me, a fissure spread all the way to my heart. Would I ever manage to break through those defenses? I wasn't sure. But if I could make even a tiny opening, that would be enough for me.

"You're quiet. That's not like you." We had been walking for a long time, dragging the remaining raptor behind us.

"I'm thinking of my brothers and sisters. I'm worried about them."

"I don't remember you having siblings."

"They're not blood relatives, but it's like they are. After I lost you I didn't have anybody. Until I met them. Evan, Simon, Ginevra . . . Gemma. They're my family."

"They're on Earth?"

I nodded. "They're all in danger." I didn't dare imagine how things had gone for them after I'd left them. "A Subterranean attacked us in our own home. That's how I ended up here."

"He killed you? Why would a Subterranean attack one of his own kind?"

"His mission is to kill Gemma. She's a mortal and her time's been up for a while now . . . but we kept Death from taking her."

"Why?"

"Because she and Evan are in love. He was the first one assigned to execute Gemma, but he disobeyed his orders and instead of killing her, he protected her. We all did."

"A mortal and a Soldier of Death? I don't know whether to call that macabre or romantic."

I smiled. "They're not the strangest couple. Ginevra's a Witch, but she's with my brother Simon, who's a Subterranean too." I shot her a look. "Come to think of it, we're missing a Damned Soul in our group. The award for couple of the year goes to you and me." I winked at her, hoping she would understand that the color of her blood didn't matter to me.

"A Witch with a Subterranean beats everything. How did she ever end up with all of you?"

"She's not like her Sisters. She's part of the family. So's Gemma. We were protecting her from the Subterraneans sent in to kill her when one of them took on the appearance of Simon during combat training. I completely fell for it. By the time I realized what was going on it was too late. If only I could get my hands on that bastard . . ." I growled, fuming. "His real target wasn't me. After he'd stabbed me he took on my appearance to brag about his plan: disguised as me, he could get close to Gemma, so killing her would be child's play. Naturally they would blame me for it." I ran my hand down my face, frustrated. "I can only hope he wasn't successful. I wish I could warn them."

"You can't," she replied coldly.

"You sure know how to comfort a guy."

"Words of comfort are an illusion. They don't change how things are. Facing the facts will make you overcome your problems more quickly."

"I don't hear any hope in your words."

"There is no hope in Hell."

Her voice was dull. I could understand why Stella had been forced to erect such an impenetrable shield around herself, but I couldn't accept that it had extinguished her spark, leaving her in a pit of darkness. I would be her fire, even at the cost of turning to ash.

Stella leaned against a boulder and unhooked a canteen from her belt. She raised it to her mouth but there was no water left.

"Thirsty?" I asked her, concerned.

She pointed to a small field of purple flowers nearby. They were almost as tall as we were and had corkscrew stems. "Those are torquinias. They contain a rich liquid composed of water and protein."

"Let's stock up, then." I took hold of one of the flowers by its stem and cut through it, but it disintegrated at my touch. I looked at Stella, raising my hands defensively. "I was gentle, I swear."

Her smile lit up her face. "It's not your fault. You can't separate a torquinia from its root. Besides, the nutrients are all right here. See?" She pushed the leaves aside to show me the little bulges on the long stalk that collected into a larger bulge at its base. "Do what I do." Stella spread the flower open and showed me the little tube inside it. She rested her lips on it, keeping her eyes steadily on mine, which had the effect of leaving me in a daze. "Be careful not to tear the petals or the flower will wither," she said, recalling my attention.

I followed her lead and soon the sweet liquid touched my mouth. It tasted good and was thirst-quenching. And yet, all I could think of at that moment was her, her eyes on mine and her lips resting on the flower, igniting my desire for her. I wished I could feel her lips against my own. I could only imagine how warm and sweet they were.

"Oh, fuck it!" I pushed the flowers aside with my arm and grabbed Stella passionately. My mouth instantly found her lips, as though it had never left them. She let herself be swept up in the moment. I pressed her back against a tree, my mind fogged by the heat of her body. She was the only thing that could satiate me. Our tongues touched and I lost myself in her, forgetting everything else. I felt delirious now that I had found her. Stella was my compass. Without her, I had lost my way. I felt every fiber of my being melting, longing to meld with her. I sank my hands into her hair to hold her tight, but Stella shoved me away.

"What the hell are you doing?" she snapped.

"You seemed to enjoy it," I said, confused.

She moved closer, her expression suddenly sensual. Resting her hand on my inner thigh, she slowly slid it up to my crotch, leaving me speechless. Before I knew it she'd snatched up one of my curved daggers and held it to my throat. "If you like your head attached, keep your distance, soldier. Not even *you* could survive without it."

"Sorry, I'm a passionate guy. I can't help it!" I winked at her and my impertinent smile annoyed her even more. She turned her back on me and started walking again. "Come on, admit it. It wasn't so bad." I had noticed how her lips had parted to welcome mine as our bodies fused with the heat of that kiss.

"You're cocky, has anyone ever told you that?"

"Lots of times, actually."

"Oh, go to hell," she snorted, picking up her pace. I grabbed her wrist and she protested. "Hey!"

"Shh." I held a finger to her lips. I had heard something. "Wait here."

I crept over to the boulder blocking our view and peered around it. Stella followed me, ignoring my instructions. In some ways she was even more stubborn than me.

When she saw the creature on the other side of the rock, a worried look spread over her face. She leaned back against the boulder and sighed. "This is all we needed, damn it."

"What's the problem? There's only one of them and we're armed to the teeth."

She looked at me as though I was raving. "That's a Molock. We have zero chance against it. Besides, there's never only one of them."

I peered out again. The enormous beast was on high alert. Its mighty buffalo hooves slowly pawed the ground and its human torso turned first to the right and then to the left as it sniffed the air, detecting our scent. I had never seen anything like it, not even in the Opalion. I definitely would have remembered an abomination like that.

Even its skin was black, like a buffalo's. Its limbs were covered with a thick reddish fur that made its way up its back and framed its face. Its chest had no fur, just a shapeless mass of frightening-looking muscles, and its deformed skull formed a pointy crown. But it was the gruesome snarl frozen on its face that gave it an absolutely loathsome appearance. With those horrible sabertooth fangs filling its mouth, the creature took the expression 'armed to the teeth' to a whole new level.

It advanced in our direction, sniffing the air through slits that moved like gills on its cheeks. I looked at the raptor I'd tied up and slung on my back. It was still bloody. "Shit. We've got to get rid of this thing."

"We should mask our scent too," Stella suggested.

I took a step back and my foot sank into a puddle of mud. "I've got an idea. Hand me your rope."

Stella did as I said. I quickly tied up the bird and hoisted it onto a branch, then took Stella's hand and guided her in the opposite direction, where the puddle of mud became a deep pit. "Ready?"

Immediately understanding my intentions, she nodded. A savage cry put us on our guard. We had to hurry.

"Don't let go of my hand," I told her before immersing us both in the filthy pit.

It was a good thing we didn't need to breathe. Still, I felt Stella's panic growing. She tightened her grip on my hand. I pressed my body against hers so she would know I was there. We had to stay hidden until the monster went away.

I couldn't see the Molock. Its hooves still shook the ground but they seemed distant. The time was right. We reemerged, totally covered with mud. There was no sign of the beast, but as a precaution we crawled back onto dry land without standing up. We were near a river, but . . . who knew if the Molock could swim?

"This way." Stella motioned for me to follow her, moving out ahead of me.

At first I didn't get what she was doing when I saw her searching through the leaves. Then I realized something was hidden among them. "What is it?"

My eyes went wide when I saw a small overturned boat.

"Our ride," she said with a smile.

All at once the ground trembled beneath us, shaken by the galloping of mighty hooves. There couldn't have been only one of them this time.

"Under the boat, quick!" I slid beneath the wooden hull and Stella followed me, our enemies' hoofbeats coming closer and closer.

"We've got to cover our scent completely! We can't let them smell us!" she warned me, urgency in her voice.

To make sure Stella was well covered with mud, I spread it over her arms, neck, and face, my hands lingering on her skin. For a second it felt like it was just her and me, hiding like children who've been playing in the mud.

But the thudding of hoofbeats soon brought me back to reality. I stretched out by her side and even held my breath. They were right there, surrounding us. Hopefully the mud and leaves wouldn't give us away. If they did, I would sacrifice myself for her, distract them so she could escape. I was ready.

Through a tiny opening I could see them as they shuffled their enormous hooves, snorting rapaciously down their long tusks. In the tense silence, Stella reached her hand through the mud and grabbed mine. I stroked it, interlaced my fingers with hers, and our eyes sought each other's. With her hand in mine, I thought I could happily have died.

A war cry burst out not far away and in reply several Molock let out a similar noise, galloping off in that direction. I heaved a sigh of relief. "They must've found that bird of ours."

Stella withdrew her hand from mine and got up. "We'd better hurry. It won't take them long to devour it."

I helped her turn the little boat right-side up and we pushed it into the water. Once inside, we lay down in the bottom to hide. The oars seemed to move on their own, almost like it was some kind of haunted craft. Once we were far from the riverbank, we sat up. The mist had covered our traces and luckily we couldn't see the shore.

"That was close," Stella said, breaking the ghostly silence. "So what do you say, now that you've had a taste of Hell?"

I folded my arms behind my head and lay down again. "Oh, it's loads of fun. Remind me to buy a ticket for my next summer vacation."

Stella laughed and wiped the mud off her face with a cloth. "Yeah, right. You'd still be in the Gluttons' den if I hadn't pulled your ass out of there. And you don't need a ticket to come back for summer vacation because you're never getting out of here."

I moved my face closer to hers, suddenly serious. "*We're* getting out of here. I'll find a way."

"No one has ever gotten out of Hell," she insisted.

Something rammed into the boat. "Brace yourself!" I shouted. Peering through the mist surrounding us, I glimpsed something gliding across the surface of the water. The creature struck the hull again and Stella let out a scream, clinging to the side of the boat. "You okay?" I shouted with concern. She nodded but squeezed her eyes shut, as though in pain.

Whatever it was, the creature was enormous and wanted to capsize us. There was nothing we could do. Our best bet was to hide and hope it went away.

"Stay down and don't move," I whispered. She did as I said. We lay on our bellies. Little by little the waves calmed and the boat stopped rocking back and forth. I raised my eyes to Stella's and found them waiting for me, close enough to probe deep into mine. For a second everything stopped and I saw nothing but her. The ink on her face brought out her eyes—and her mouth. The yearning to touch her lips with mine became almost painful.

A series of grunts checked my impulse. I scowled. Every time I got close to Stella, Hell got between us. Would we ever be safe?

It was up to me to check whether we had run into some other danger. I slowly raised my head and instantly ducked down again, wishing I hadn't looked in the first place. What I'd seen on the bank were Souls devouring each other, tearing the flesh off each other like zombies. They were the Insane, the only kind of Souls in Hell who had lost every trace of their humanity. They fed off raw flesh or—even worse—still-living creatures. They were an abomination but, unlike in the movies, weren't brainless, bloodthirsty creatures. Instead, they were sly and dangerous. I would never allow Stella to lose her humanity and turn into one of those creatures. I would get her out of there. I stroked her cheek and she let me, still gazing into my eyes.

The boat banged into something. We flinched, thinking it was the swamp creature again. Instead it was a rock close to shore. I jumped into the water, which reached my chest. "Quick, we've got to swim to shore before that thing comes back."

Stella ignored the hand I was holding out to her, though, and leapt onto the rock. She caught hold of a branch sticking out over the water and climbed onto it.

"Or you could do it your way," I said, watching her as she pulled herself up into the tree.

She jumped down onto the shore. "Is it going to take you much longer?"

I smiled. Now she was teasing me. We'd made progress. I dove into the water to swim to her but suddenly let myself sink beneath the surface. I flailed my arms as if struggling to stay afloat.

"Drake!"

Intermittently I saw Stella on the shore, anxiously keeping her bow and arrow trained in my direction, prepared to shoot the creature the second it emerged. I shot up to the surface with a big grin on my face.

"So you do care about me a little."

Stella glowered, not enjoying my prank. "You're a real idiot."

I got out of the water, dripping wet. "And you're really sexy when you worry about me."

"If you want a punch in the face you're heading in the right direction."

"You already hurt me, and bad, when you didn't dive in to save me."

"You need to learn to save yourself." Stella started walking again, her pace brisk.

"Come on, I thought you wanted to kid around. You started it." I tried to stop her but she pulled away.

"Don't touch me. You're wet."

"What, you afraid of a little water?" The smile died on my lips when I saw the burns on her arm. "Hold on, how did you get these?" I grabbed her wrist to get a closer look at her new injuries.

"The water's full of poison. The Damned can't go into it without getting burned. You, on the other hand, don't have a scratch on you. Another privilege you Subterraneans have on top of being immortal." There was resentment in her voice. If I could have given her my immortality I would have done it on the spot.

It had been stupid of me. The water had stung my skin, but the pure venom of the Witches' serpents had been injected into me so many times through their bites that a relatively low concentration like the one in the river was no problem for me. "You're wrong. Subterraneans' skin isn't immune to poison. Mine's just gotten used to it."

Her eyes shot to mine when she seemed to understand. She wasn't the only one who had been through hell.

"Here we are." Stella pushed aside some branches, pulled back a log, and the rock in front of us moved, revealing the entrance to a cave.

"What is this place?" I asked, surprised.

Stella smiled at me. "Welcome to my home."

7

SWEET POISON

"You can relax. We're safe here," Stella said as I tried to make out my surroundings through the darkness. She lit a strange light and the cave glowed faintly, showing me her smile. She seemed comfortable, as though she were used to bringing people here.

Tongues of fire spread along a groove carved into the ground, lighting up the whole room. It wasn't very spacious but it lacked nothing. In one corner was a small table and two chairs carved into the rock. There was even a small fireplace and a well into which water was trickling.

Thick fur pelts covered a large sleeping pallet. I threw myself onto it. "Oof! Less comfortable than it looks." From there something caught my eye: an axe hung on the wall in a niche of the cave I hadn't seen at first. I moved closer and was left openmouthed. It was packed with weapons. Stella had an arsenal. I stepped into the space, studying the walls:

there were knives in all shapes and sizes, spears carved from wood, war hammers, arrows, and even devices I didn't recognize. Some were crude, others unfinished.

I heard her footsteps approaching. "Did you make all these weapons?" I asked.

"Learning to defend yourself takes patience."

"And I figured you were a damsel in distress."

Stella took an arrow from the wall, examined its head, and began to sharpen it. "You were wrong."

"I can see that. I'm happy you've gotten to be so strong," I admitted. Our eyes met. "Otherwise, given what I've seen of Hell, you wouldn't have survived all this time."

"You haven't seen anything of Hell yet," she said grimly.

She took off her weapons belt and rested it on the stone counter along with her bow and arrows and a series of daggers that had been hidden here and there on her toned body. I stared at her the whole time, one eyebrow raised. She was armed to the teeth. When I thought she was done, she pulled out long, sharp pins from her hair. Finally, she placed what looked like small white stones on the counter.

"What are those?"

"My secret weapon." She winked, grinning at me for the first time.

Stella turned and took something else down from the wall. I recognized them at once: they were two long black beaks like the ones on the raptors we had encountered, only they were bound together. Stella spread them open to show me how they worked. She had devised a pair of scissors.

"Brilliant," I said, looking them over.

"You can use them to get all that hair off your face, if you like."

I distractedly touched my beard. I hadn't shaved since I'd gotten to Hell. My hair had grown pretty long too.

Stella disappeared for a moment and came back with two small rudimentary bowls, one with water and the other full of a reddish gel, which she set down next to me.

"Where are you going?" I asked as she walked toward a narrow opening in the wall.

"I need to get this mud off my clothes," she said. She disappeared, leaving me alone to grapple with the razor-sharp gadget.

"Can't be that hard," I muttered to myself. I had never tried shaving without a mirror before, but I'd handled worse weapons when drunk, so— I took a dab of the gel from the bowl and spread it over my jaw. It puffed up on my skin, forming a thick red foam, so thick I could barely see. "Stella, you sure this gel isn't going to eat my face?"

To my surprise, I heard her laugh. She was nearby, her voice loud and clear. "It's shevad, a disinfectant foam I make from flower extract. It won't eat you, you have my word."

"If you say so." With a shrug, I wiped a bit of it off and rested the blade on my face.

"Drake?" A knot formed in my stomach when I heard her say my name. "Earlier, when you were battling the raptors, you said you'd fought in the Opalion. Did you really?"

"Yeah."

Stella was silent for a moment. "I watched the Games

once. They're brutal." I nodded, as though she could see me. "Were you subjugated to one of them?"

The blade came to a halt against my skin. She was talking about the Witches.

My hesitation made her change the subject. "How did you manage to escape from the Castle? And what makes you think they won't come looking for you?"

I smiled. She had never said so much all at once before. "I don't think they care about me, really. There are thousands of Subterraneans at the Castle. My bet is they don't even notice I'm gone." I put down the scissors and went over to the opening in the wall through which Stella had disappeared. "I'm coming in," I warned her. I didn't want to risk finding her naked and ending up with another arrow in my chest.

Her silence encouraged me to go in. I crossed through the narrow passageway and couldn't believe my eyes. The opening expanded into a grotto inside of which was a small lake lit by small, smooth objects that looked like luminescent stones floating here and there on its surface. Stella was kneeling at the water's edge, washing her clothes.

When she saw me she stopped and looked up at me steadily. I hadn't only shaved off my beard. I'd also gotten rid of my long hair, giving myself a crew cut like the one I'd had when we first met. I wanted to remind her that it was still me, the soldier she had fallen in love with. At the very least I was hoping to inspire a specific emotion in her: a sweet memory. Judging from her expression, it had worked.

Stella stood up, looking shaken. She hung her clothes up to dry and walked over to me. I tried not to think about the fact that she was naked beneath the cloth wrapped around her. She still had mud on her arms and her face was still covered with ink.

I stroked her arm, examining her skin. It was smooth again. There were no new burn marks, even though she had just washed her clothes. "Why doesn't this water burn you like it did at the river?"

Instead of pulling back, she interlaced her fingers with mine. "Come, I'll show you." Squeezing her hand, I felt the energy she instilled in me spread through my body.

She led me down a path that made its way to the back of the lake. The passageway gradually grew narrower as the water got deeper and finally came to a dead end.

"If you wanted to drown me, you could have done it when we were in the boat," I joked.

Her soft laughter echoed off the grotto walls. "Relax, I don't want to kill you."

I studied the rock in front of us, fascinated. It glimmered with silvery reflections, almost like it was a piece of the moon that had fallen off. "What are we doing here, then?"

"You'll see." Stella pulled a lever and I heard the sound of a trapdoor opening, followed by a soft gurgle that came closer and closer. Finally, a stream of water flowed into the lake, quickly raising the surface level. Stella took something from the wall and held it to her face. It was a rudimentary mask made of thick leather. Several of them hung from the wall. She handed me one and gestured for me to put it on. "It's a little small, but it should be enough."

It was hard to see her with that contraption on my face. What was she going to do?

The answer came soon enough. She picked up a stick and scraped its tip against the ceiling until the silvery dust coating the rock collected on it. With a flick of her wrist she scratched it against the wall and the improvised torch flamed up.

"Whoa!" I instinctively pulled back at the sudden burst of heat that touched my face. Stella ignored me and lowered the torch to the lake. The flames caressed the water, running across its surface like a mantle of silk.

I lowered my mask to get a better look at the dazzling display of lights before my eyes. The grotto had become a kaleidoscope of colors as red, blue, and purple danced over the lake, peeking between the flames. Stella took my mask and put it back over my face, shooting me a look of disapproval.

The fire died out and a thick cloud drifted into the air. There was something strange about the mist. It seemed to be glowing. It rose all the way to the ceiling and the rocky surface shimmered, filling the grotto with a silvery light. What was going on?

"Move, quick!" Stella darted around me toward a crank hidden in the corner. She began to turn it over and over, unfurling a cloth wrapped around a tree trunk over our heads. It was a patchwork—fur, for the most part—and it slid along thin tracks dug into the walls so it wouldn't fall as it spread open.

"You could give me a hand instead of loafing around." Hearing the urgency in Stella's voice, I rushed to act, but when I began to help her she laughed. "Just kidding. I can manage on my own." Even so, she let me turn the crank with her. "Okay, that's enough." She stopped and took off her mask. The cloth now covered the entire grotto, inches from the ceiling.

"What the heck is that thing?"

"It's my water purification system," she said proudly. "These rocks are porous and they filter the water that comes in. A small amount of poison still manages to get through, so I created channels to control the flow of the water. When I ignite its surface all the poison evaporates and settles on the walls and ceiling." With her stick she scraped off another bit of the silvery dust and showed it to me. "It'd be a shame to waste so much poison, don't you think?" It looked like a silver scepter in the hands of a true queen of the Underworld.

"Your arrow . . ." I touched the wound on my chest. That was why Stella's arrow had put me out of action: it had been poisoned. I had just had confirmation of that. "It's brilliant," I said, fascinated.

"Survival instinct," she replied. Then she smiled, proud of her work. "I collect poison to defend myself, but also to find food. It didn't take me long to realize that poison could be a resource. What can kill me can also kill my enemies. Arrows, daggers, traps. Everything is much more dangerous when it's poisoned."

"It's not a good idea to pick a fight with you, then."

"By the time my enemies realize that, it's usually too late." Stella laughed. I wished she would keep laughing for hours. "In powder form the poison is less dangerous and harder to use. You need to scrape it off, heat it up, and melt it down. With time I learned to concoct a lethal solution, but you need lots of powder to make even a few drops of it. That's why this is a job that needs to be done every day."

Stella dropped the cloth covering her and dove into the water, leaving me stunned. "Are you just going to stand there or are you going to come in and get cleaned up?" she teased me when she emerged from the water.

"You sure? I can wait until you're finished, if you want."

What the hell was wrong with me?

"I'm not going to ask you a second time."

"I won't wait to be asked twice," I murmured to myself. I pulled off my pants and dove in, emerging beside her. "All this poison kind of goes to your head, don't you think?"

"Are you trying to take advantage of me?" she replied, her expression teasing.

God, was she beautiful. "I'm afraid you'll be the one to take advantage of *me*."

For a moment everything seemed to stop as the silvery grotto whirled around us. Stella's eyes were locked on mine. The luminous stones glimmered on the water. I was adrift in an ocean of stars and she was my comet.

She cautiously reached out her hand and stroked my shaved head, her gaze lost in distant thoughts. What I would have given to be able to read her mind just then. The water was scalding hot and steam rose up all around us. It didn't glitter like the steam permeated with poison, but I felt intoxicated simply because she was there, so close to me.

"Do you still remember your past?" I asked her, afraid of her answer.

"Not always," she replied. She sounded sincere.

"What about when you found me? Did you know who I

was?" She shook her head regretfully. "Why did you save me, then?"

"Because you knew who *I* was. Sometimes I'm not even sure I know who I used to be. I'm forgetting. It had been so long since anyone had said my name. Then you showed up. The memories connected to my life on Earth come and go, and I feel like I'm losing them."

"You said you'd dreamed about me," I suddenly remembered. Maybe deep down she still cared for me.

"Everything has been so confused lately. But not the dreams. Those have always been clear."

"Do you dream about us on Earth?"

She shook her head. "I dream about you here in Hell." The revelation disturbed me, but I kept it to myself. "When I found you I knew you'd been a part of my life, but the memories of that Stella are fading and soon I'll lose them forever. That's what happens before you cross over to the other side."

"What other side?" I asked hesitantly.

"The more my memories fade, the more I risk becoming one of the Insane. And if there's one thing I fear more than death, it's that."

"It'll never happen. I won't let it."

Stella looked into my eyes. "I get closer to the edge every day."

I couldn't stand seeing her so frightened. I moved closer and brushed the hair away from her face. "Not any more, now that I'm here. Of course you're a bit bolder than you were the last time I saw you, my little savage, but I never said I didn't like it," I admitted, getting a smile out of her.

Hell drove Souls to self-annihilation, turning them into creatures who were increasingly worthy of being there. I had seen some transform before my eyes. Their stares went blank when their very last trace of humanity vanished and they became zombies. Their eyes went pitch black. I drove off the memories before Stella could read them on my face. I would never let that happen to her. At the Castle, even I had risked losing myself. Finding each other again had saved us both.

Stella smiled and her face lit up. "That's what I liked about you the most: the way you always made everything seem so simple."

"You're wrong. What you liked the most was when I would flex my muscles at you. It made you forget your problems." I flexed my bicep to get her to laugh again. I didn't want her to stop. It worked, and the grotto filled with the melody.

"All of a sudden I'm remembering how arrogant you were, too." She swam away.

I swam after her. "Nothing else?"

"You were presumptuous, insolent, and more than a bit cocky."

"You're forgetting funny, passionate, and, most important, gorgeous."

"Yes, a gorgeous bag of hot air."

I laughed with her, hoping the moment would never end, but Stella grew serious again. She came closer and rested her hand on my left arm, studying the symbols branded on my skin, the marks that had condemned me. "How did you become a Soldier of Death?"

"During World War II, you know, I was a pilot in the U.S. armed forces. I'd been granted a furlough. I wanted to come home to you. Two days before I was scheduled to go, we were flying in hostile territory when an enemy squad attacked us. I managed to shake them and bring the plane down safely, but they'd hit me. When I landed, I remember thinking I would never see you again." I brushed my fingers against the dog tag around my neck and gripped it in my fist, reliving those terrible moments. Not terrible because I had lost my life—I hadn't been afraid of dying—but because at that very instant I lost Stella. "A Witch was there waiting for me," I added. "Kreeshna. She wanted to take me with her to Hell, but another Subterranean chased her off. Since then, Evan has been like a brother to me."

"So that's why you helped protect his human girlfriend." I nodded. "I'm sorry you're trapped here and can't help them any more," she said.

"If I had known you were in Hell I would've followed that Witch here in 1941." But I hadn't, and Stella had ended up all alone and in danger that whole time. "I'm sorry."

"You couldn't have known," she reassured me, seeing the agony on my face.

"On that last mission I was distracted. I couldn't wait for it to end so I could get back to you. I wanted to give you this." I took the dog tag from around my neck and turned it in my fingers, embittered by the past that had been stolen from me. "It wasn't much, but I wanted you to know how much you meant to me."

"You can give it to me now."

My eyes shot to hers. Stella pushed her hair to the side, encouraging me with her gaze. I moved closer to her until I felt her breath on my skin. "You're not going to shoot me with another arrow?" I asked softly. I placed the dog tag around her neck and paused, suddenly incapable of moving away from her, of doing without the warmth of her breath so close to me.

She didn't push me away. Instead she rested her hands on my chest. "I'll try not to," she replied in a whisper. I watched her lips curve into a slight smile. The yearning to touch them with mine was driving me wild. I brought my mouth to her neck, but didn't touch it. I wanted to inhale my fill of her scent, so familiar to me. With my lips I brushed her shoulder, her chin, her cheek, and finally, nuzzled her nose with mine.

"I've missed you so much." Our bodies were drawn to each other like magnets. A stronger force had held us apart up to that moment, but I was no longer willing to submit to that force.

"Drake," she murmured, and brushed her lips against mine. Their warmth clouded my mind. It felt like I had been waiting for that moment for centuries. I grabbed Stella by the nape and pulled her to me, melding with her. I clasped her bottom and lifted her up, pushing her back against the wall. She surrendered, neither of us able to resist the hidden connection that united us, a connection she could no longer deny. I felt it in the warmth of her skin. I sensed it in her nails on my back, clamped so tightly I couldn't move away. She was mine. She always had been. I entered her and her heat washed over me, surrounded me, annihilated me. I kissed her neck, trembling uncontrollably. She whispered my name, driving me wild.

Nothing could have matched the beauty of that moment, the emotions surging through me. I had been dead inside; only now did I realize it. My world had lost all its color. Finding Stella again had changed everything. It had changed me. I gripped her bottom and held her even closer as the grotto filled with her voice passionately calling my name and I exploded inside her. A tear slid silently down my cheek.

I continued to kiss her neck, nibbling it gently. "I'll get you out of here," I promised. She smiled. Our eyes found each other, just as they had in 1941.

Heaven wasn't so far away after all.

8

THE QUEEN OF HELL

The poison glimmered on the dark walls like stardust. The grotto was illuminated here and there by the glowing stones floating on the surface of the tiny private lake. Stella was still there, clinging to me, like a dream that would never fade. She had tried to swim away but I'd kept her close. I wasn't about to let her get away from me. I wasn't about to lose her ever again.

Her gaze rested on the scar on my eyebrow. She knew it was a gift from Hell. She touched it with her finger. "I can't do anything about this."

I smiled. Her instincts as a Red Cross volunteer hadn't changed. "It doesn't matter. You've healed a much deeper wound." I took her hand and drew it to my chest. "Right here." I had been through hell with the Witches, but it was all forgotten now that she was with me.

"Were you with other women while I was gone?" she asked all at once.

"No one who mattered." It was the truth. I'd had lots of women, but none of them had ever meant anything to me. My heart had always belonged to her.

"So yes," she replied with a sly glance.

I stroked the wound on my chest. "You've already shot me once. We'd better not dredge up the past too much."

"Relax, big talker. Angry jealousy is for the weak."

"Lucky me, then," I joked.

Stella shook her head. "You must be a terrible catch."

"I've been told that too," I admitted. Her laughter filled the grotto. I held her tight, watching the rhythmic shimmering of the rocks on the lake.

"Maybe this is all just a dream. A mirage generated by madness," she said.

"If it is, then I've gone crazy too. But never, ever do I want to be cured of you," I whispered against her neck. Stella smelled like fruit, an exotic scent I could never get enough of. I sank my nose into her hair and she smiled.

"That tickles. Stop it."

Her examination of me wasn't over. It was as if she was renewing her memory of my body by discovering what had changed. She studied the tattoo on my arm as I gently nibbled her golden skin. Her fingers stopped on my chest, tracing another scar, one left by Kreeshna: the mark of her poisoned fingernails. "You never answered my question," she said, her voice turning somber. "Were you subjugated to a Witch?"

"A Witch tried to use her charms on me, but you're the

one who's bewitched me." I tried to nibble her earlobe but she pushed me away.

"I'm serious. Have you drunk their blood?"

"I'm not a filthy vampire." I sniffed her neck and slowly bit it.

"Seems like you're practicing to become one right now," she joked.

"Seems like you're a willing victim." I stroked her arms, enjoying the shivers of pleasure I could tell I caused in her. Pressed against mine, her naked body sent the blood rushing to my brain. "God, are you sexy."

"There are no gods down here."

"A goddess, yes. I'm looking at her right now."

"You're confusing me with the ones at the Castle."

"They aren't goddesses. They're the foulest of harpies."

"And yet you must've had lots of fun with the queens of Hell. I've heard they're a bunch of capricious bitches in heat." She locked her eyes on mine. It almost sounded like . . .

"You jealous, my little savage?" A smile escaped me.

She pushed me away and turned to swim off, but I stopped her. "Hold it. Where do you think you're going?"

"Far from your stupid insinuations. I have no reason to be jealous. And wipe that dumb grin off your face."

"I can't. This is too funny."

Stella sulked. "Always the big talker. Why didn't you stay with them if you were having such a good time?"

I forced her to look at me. The smile had disappeared from my lips. "They were after you. That was enough to make me escape."

She frowned for a moment, confused by what I had said, but a second later her expression grew serious again. "You should've stayed at the Castle. You were safer there. It's more dangerous than you think out here."

I brushed the hair away from her face. "Survival is easier when there are two of us."

"I've gotten by just fine on my own."

"I wasn't talking about you."

"You shouldn't have come," she insisted. "You were crazy to do it."

"The longer I spent at the Castle, the more I risked forgetting who I was. But when I found out you were here I didn't hesitate. Letting you slip through my fingers is the only act of insanity I've ever committed."

Stella swallowed and looked at me steadily, her expression hard. "The Stella you knew is dead."

She seemed convinced of what she was saying. I was the one who didn't want to accept it. "No. I refuse to believe that. She's still here. She just has a little ink on her face, that's all." I ran my thumb over her cheek, removing the last traces of color. It was like seeing her again for the first time. Hell had changed her, but behind her warrior façade she was still there waiting for me. I could only imagine what she'd had to endure without me . . . I would never forgive myself for that.

Her dark, intense eyes penetrated me, touching my soul. All at once the idea of having survived on Earth without her seemed insane. That had been my true hell.

I interlaced my fingers with hers. "I just fell in love with you for the third time," I whispered.

She looked puzzled. "When was the second?"

"When you shot me with that arrow, isn't it obvious?" I winked at her and she laughed, but a noise in the next room put us on our guard. "What was that?"

"I'll go check," she said at once, but I stopped her.

"You stay. I'll go." Though she seemed reluctant to do as I said, she didn't follow me.

I climbed out of the pool and advanced cautiously. Someone was in the cave. Given the rustling noise echoing off the walls, there was no doubt about it. At the water's edge I put on my pants and picked up a large rock. When I went into the main room, though, the noise stopped. No one was there.

Worried, I looked around. They must have hidden.

Gripping my weapon tightly in my fist, I advanced slowly and almost tripped over something. I didn't know Stella's cave very well, but I was sure the big rock in the middle of the room hadn't been there before. I tried to push it aside with my foot, but it was too heavy.

I went back to call Stella. "Everything's fine. Nobody's —" Before I could finish my sentence something charged me like a battering ram, slamming me against the wall.

"What the hell?" I gasped, holding my stomach. It had been the rock. It wasn't an inanimate object. It had opened up like a hedgehog and attacked me.

Stella came in, her bow readied, and scanned the room. I gestured toward the strange creature, which now busy gnawing on something. Instead of shooting the enemy, she lowered her weapon and walked over to the animal.

"Stop! It's dangerous!" I warned her. Like she would listen to me anyway.

She got down on all fours and caught its attention. The stone hedgehog turned and prepared to charge at her.

"Stella, look out!"

It leapt on top of her. I tensed, but she burst out laughing. *It was tickling her.* "Calm down, Drake. It's just Tricu."

The animal jumped down and came over to me. It was similar to the thing I had come across right outside the Castle, just a lot smaller. It sniffed me, jerking its head all over until it found what it was looking for. Snatching the rock out of my hand, it turned around to munch on it.

"What the hell is that thing?"

"He's a Gork. And don't worry, he's harmless."

"Tell that to my stomach," I grumbled, still aching. "I didn't think I would ever say this, but he's even uglier than Iron Dog."

"Iron Dog? What's that?"

"A rat with a pig's tail." Tricu, on the other hand, was a cross between a hedgehog and a teddy bear.

"What a strange creature," she mused.

I laughed. "I always said so too, but my friends thought I was nuts."

"Do you miss them?"

"I miss you."

Stella looked away, becoming cold again.

I was an idiot. I had to give her time to get used to me. By breathing down her neck I only risked driving her away. But there was nothing I could do about it. Patience had never been my forte.

Not wanting her to stop talking to me, I went back to safer ground. She seemed to like the stone hedgehog/teddy bear. It was a good topic. "So what is he, some sort of house pet?"

That got a smile out of her. "More or less."

"You must be joking! Haven't you seen how big they get when they grow up? Not to mention their breath! I ran into a giant one in the forest." I still remembered the deafening shriek it had blown in my face.

"Size is an advantage, if he's on your side." Stella let out a whistle. On her command, Tricu turned to look at us. He grew bigger and bigger until he touched the ceiling of the cave. He opened his jaws and let out something that sounded like a yawn, then moved his snout toward me and began to nip at me, pinning me to the wall.

Stella laughed. "Don't worry, he's not going to eat you. Gorks don't eat meat, just rocks."

"You sure about that? He doesn't seem to like me very much."

She shrugged. "Well, he might munch on a few of your bones."

"What?!" I said, shocked. I tried to break free, but the beast was enormous and there was no way to push him aside.

"Relax. For now he's just cuddling you." When Stella whistled again, the teddy-bear rock pulled away from me and grew smaller again. I covered my face with my arm as a cascade of pebbles scattered through the room.

"It's always the same old story. You're not the first little monster to hate me, you know?" I told him. Gemma's pet, Iron Dog, hated my guts.

"It was Tricu who led me to you in the Gluttons' cave. His grunt got my attention." The beast let out a yelp, which echoed off the walls.

"Speaking of which, you should buy him some mints." His breath was pestilential. In his defense, rocks can't have been easy to digest.

The Gork went over to the entrance and came back wagging his tail. Something was in his jaws. "What've you got there?" I asked. The animal dropped four rodents at my feet.

"Our dinner," Stella replied with a smile.

Just then, a drop of water fell from the ceiling and landed on Tricu, followed by another. The animal let out an annoyed growl and began to shake himself like a wet dog.

Stella's eyes went wide. "Look out!" she cried, warning me, but it was too late. A shower of pebbles shot toward us like bullets. I turned to Stella and covered her body with mine while my back was machine-gunned. She let me shield her, hiding in my arms.

When Tricu finished shaking, my eyes locked with hers. "I'm sorry," she said softly, inches from my face.

"It was worth it," I said with a wink. I would have let myself be hit by a thousand stones if it meant I could be this close to her.

Stella cleared her throat and changed the subject. "We'd better go out and get some firewood. Those rats need to be cooked. Unless you want to share Tricu's food, that is."

"My stomach's been through enough for today. Better

rats than rocks." I shook my head. I would never have imagined saying something like that.

Stella took out a large pot and filled it with water from the well in the middle of the room. "Do you like stew?"

I smiled at her. "I've had worse. You stay here. I'll go out and get the firewood."

"Wait." She rummaged around in a chest and tossed me something. "Put this on."

It was a green sleeveless shirt. "Why do you have men's clothes in your house?"

"None of your business."

I didn't like her answer. "Where'd you get it?" I insisted.

"Just put it on, Drake."

I grumbled. I would find out later. "Afraid of giving in to temptation?" I asked her, grinning.

She rolled her eyes. "Do what you want, but if I were you I wouldn't go around half-naked. Hell is a dangerous enough place even without all the infernal creatures."

"Or I'm too good-looking and you're afraid you won't be able to resist me. Again," I teased her, one eyebrow raised.

"Hurry up, you idiot, before I eat these rats raw."

"You wouldn't dare."

Stella shot me a sly look. "Don't try me."

"Okay, I'll go get the wood. You, don't pull any pranks." I put on the shirt and moved the rock blocking the entrance to one side, wondering how Tricu had managed to slip inside. It wasn't a big mystery, actually, since he could change size.

The cool air of Hell hit me full in the face. The cave was

much warmer and the change in temperature gave me goosebumps. "Good thing I'm wearing this shirt," I said to myself. Or maybe it was the idea of leaving Stella all alone that had given me goosebumps. I had to hurry. I made my way into the Copse and picked up a long stick. I broke it into smaller pieces and went looking for others.

A sudden noise made me freeze. I scanned the forest with my eyes. Who knew what monsters were lurking in the eternal twilight. It happened again: the sound of a twig snapping. I spun around and he was in front of me. A Damned Soul. We stared hard at each other. He didn't move a muscle, but his dark eyes probed mine. His head was shaved on both sides. In the center was a crest of dark hair that he had braided and bound into a ponytail. It looked like he was just a kid, but I knew he wasn't.

The Soul tilted his head to the side, sneered, and vanished as swiftly as a ghost. My eyes chased him: a black patch darting through the forest. I dropped the firewood, grabbed a thick stick, whirled around, and struck my adversary, thwarting his attempt to attack me from behind. I was well aware of how Souls like him operated. I had faced lots of them in the Opalion.

He crashed to the ground, caught off guard by my speed, but he didn't leave me with the upper hand for long. Nimbly shooting to his feet, he grabbed another one of the sticks.

"Hey, those are for dinner."

The Soul attacked me, black blood oozing from his cheek. Maybe he didn't speak my language, but one thing was clear: to him, *I* was dinner. I dodged his blows and counterattacked, quickly bringing the duel to an end. He was strong, but I had been trained for combat, first during the war and later—even more gruelingly—at the Witches' Castle, where battles to the death had forged me. I blocked his stick with mine and disarmed him. Shoving him back against a tree, I pressed the weapon to his throat. He glared at me defiantly. He didn't look like someone who had just been defeated.

"Okay, buddy, I don't mean to eat you. If you promise to do the same, I'll let you go."

A sneer spread over his face. "We're the ones who won't let *you* go."

He could speak.

Frowning, I heard a rustling noise. My head shot up. A group of Souls leapt down from the trees, their drawn bows aimed at me. The kid wasn't alone. And I was surrounded.

I shoved him away and raised my fists, preparing to take them on. I tried to count them with my eyes. They were everywhere. With a shrug, I smiled. "I've dealt with worse." I hurled my stick at one of them like a spear, but a barrage of arrows smashed it away before it could hit him.

Two Souls attacked me together. I regretted not having brought any knives with me. Fortunately I was fast. I snatched an arrow from one of them and stabbed him with it full in the chest. Grabbing his dagger, I turned to face the other one, but found his arrow pointed right at my face.

"You know I can't die, don't you?"

To my surprise, the man replied, "Remind me of that when you're inside my belly." He drew his bow tauter and aimed at my throat.

"Stop!" A voice thundered through the clearing. It was Stella.

"Shit," I murmured. I gestured with my dagger as a warning to the Soul not to move. "Stella! Get out of here!" I shouted.

Instead, she continued to advance toward me . . . and everyone lowered their weapons. I looked around in bewilderment as the Damned knelt down, one by one. Only the Soul whose arrow was aimed at me didn't move a muscle.

Stella spoke again, this time in the language of the Damned, and my adversary answered her. She came toward us and everyone moved aside to let her pass. Once beside me, she and the Damned Soul who had remained standing stared at each other for a long moment. He was the only one who hadn't lowered his weapon. He had dark hair that partially covered his face and looked like an ex-con.

In a gesture of peace Stella slid her two daggers into the sheaths on her thigh. "He's with me," she announced, her tone stern. After a moment of hesitation, the Soul lowered his bow.

"What does all this mean?" I asked.

Stella smiled at me. "It means that out here *I'm* the queen."

9

SENSATIONS OF TIMES PAST

"What do you mean, you're the queen? And what the hell did you two say to each other? I don't know your language."

"I told them not to kill you—for now." Stella turned her back on me and walked toward the cave, all the others following closely behind.

"Your subjects aren't very hospitable." I looked over my shoulder. She might trust them, but that didn't mean I would. The kid I'd battled glared at me bitterly. I clenched my fists when he got a little too close to Stella. I was about to stop him, but she rested her hand on his arm and whispered something in his ear. He nodded and shot me another dirty look as he helped Stella unsling her bow from her shoulder. There was something I didn't like about the way they were standing so close.

"Didn't you say people don't bond around here?" I

asked, striding over to her. I watched the tribe of men and
women moving around outside the entrance to Stella's hideaway and settling in. They seemed to be planning to stay.

"I haven't bonded with any of them."

"Could've fooled me," I shot back sourly. Stella followed
my eyes to the kid, who was busy sharpening a long knife.
"He's a bit more attentive toward you than the others, don't
you think?"

"That's Vargan, son of the great chief of the Grimash.
We have an alliance."

"Since when?"

"Since I killed his father. It's a long story and it's none of
your business." Stella moved closer until she was inches
away from my face. "Listen, the Copse is a dangerous place.
There are forces better left unchallenged, and others that
are better controlled."

"What do you mean?"

"I mean that even if you can't trust anyone, it's wise to
have allies. So calm down, soldier. This side of the river is
my territory. Like I told you, we're safe."

"Why are they here? And how long are they going
to stay?"

"Until all the others arrive. Meanwhile—"

"Meanwhile what?"

Drums began to beat with a tribal rhythm and Stella
smiled at me. "We enjoy the party." I returned her smile and
looked around. A fire came to life in the center of the clearing, lighting everything up as the men broke into a crude
dance.

"Coming with me?" Stella asked.

"Where?"

She handed me my daggers. "Those rats won't be enough for all these people." She leapt into the air and grabbed hold of a branch. With a flip she pulled herself up. I flashed her a smile, but it faded when I saw Vargan hold out his hand to her from the uppermost branch. I grunted. Usually I liked threesomes, but not if Stella was involved.

"Would you rather wait for us here?" she said, egging me on.

I took a running start and jumped up to grab hold of the branch. "No, I'd rather follow you guys and rip his head off with my bare hands," I muttered to myself.

Two other Souls accompanied us: a man with black skin and a woman with Asian features. As I struggled to keep up with them, I discovered they were called Lus and Ada. I was accustomed to battles and would have defined myself as the athletic type, but they were all moving through the trees as swiftly as monkeys. They seemed like natives who had grown up in the jungle, especially Stella, at the head of the group. From time to time one of them would come to a sudden halt and shoot an arrow. A moment later they would return with a new kill.

Stella stopped on a large branch and I rushed to her side before her wingman could. Only in my fighter plane had I ever been so high up.

"Drake, look," she said, her eyes filled with wonder.

In the distance, the sky was a sheet of black crystal fractured by a thousand bright cracks that snaked across it like branches with our every breath, illuminating everything. They were lightning bolts, a sight as frightening as it was exhilarating, no doubt generated by the Witches. Some-where in the middle of all that, the Castle was hidden. I held back a shudder and impulsively slipped my hand into Stella's.

"It's time to get back," Vargan said. "We have what we need." He stared at me hard and I interlaced my fingers with Stella's, making sure he noticed. It was better to set things straight right from the start.

"Fine." Stella fastened her prey to her belt. "Let's get back to the camp." She let go of my hand, looked at me, and flung herself into empty space, arms outstretched.

"Stella!" I screamed, lurching forward as I tried to grab her. Vargan sneered at me and followed Stella's example, as did all the others. "Fuck," I muttered, and jumped. I didn't know what was below us, but if they had done it, there was no way I wasn't going to follow them. I plunged into the abyss and immediately made out something through the twilight: a thick network of vines growing from trees so tall they seemed to be dangling from the sky. Stella's laughter echoed through the Copse, filling me with energy. I caught a vine and swung through the air until I reached another one and yet another. It was electrifying. When I got close to Stella, I let go of my vine and grabbed hers.

"Drake!" she exclaimed with surprise, but then she smiled at me.

"If I didn't know where we were, I would swear this was Heaven," I whispered against her lips. I held her close and she looked into my eyes as the air gently rocked us in its embrace. Feeling her lips so close was a form of sweet madness that went straight to my head. I'd barely brushed them with mine when the vine suddenly snapped, sending us plunging down. I held Stella in my arms until we had rolled to a halt on the ground.

"What the hell?" I groaned, aching from the impact. "Stella, you okay?" She nodded.

"Nice landing," Vargan said. There was a chorus of laughter. We were back at the camp. I caught sight of his boomerang-knife a second before he put it away to help Stella. He challenged me with his eyes as he took her hand and held it in his. That sly smirk spoke volumes. It was he who had made us fall.

I leapt to my feet and faced him, slamming my hands into his chest. "She could've gotten hurt."

"Then you shouldn't have taken her so far up," he shot back, inches from my face.

"Hey, hey! What's going on?" Stella stepped between us and made us back off each other. Then she leaned closer to me. "Drake, I told you to calm down. We're all on the same side here."

"Well, maybe he's a little too much on yours."

Stella held my gaze and then said something to the kid. I couldn't stand her being so close to him. Or their talking in Grimtholk, for that matter. When she walked away, the Soul smiled and passed me, bumping my shoulder as he did. "So that's where my shirt was."

A surge of blood clouded my mind and I lost control.

"Drake! Drake, stop! Let him go!"

I barely heard Stella's voice as I held Vargan pinned to a tree, ready to rip the smile off his face. "She's with me," I hissed, almost like it was an order.

Vargan glared back at me, then looked over my shoulder. I turned too, and saw Stella. She cast me a bitter glance and walked away.

The other Souls seemed to be having fun. Some of them moved to the beat of the drums, doing cartwheels, flips, and acrobatic leaps from high in the trees. Others had captured an Insane Soul and were having a competition to see who could hit him from a distance with arrows and knives while he writhed against a tree trunk. Another group, including Stella, was gathered around the fire.

I spotted a face I recognized and went up to him, slapping my hands on his big shoulders. "Gurdan! You're back!"

He gripped my fist and to my surprise pulled me against him in a man hug. "Still one piece, Princess."

Out of the corner of my eye I noticed Stella smiling at the sight. "Don't hug me so hard or I won't be for long," I gasped. His grip was bone-crushing. When Gurdan let go of me I went over to Stella and sat down beside her. In her hands was a bowl. She was busy grinding up its contents. It was thick and black. "What is that stuff?" I asked.

She got up and sat down facing me, her legs crossed and the bowl between us. "Want me to show you?"

I nodded, my eyes locked on hers. I wasn't used to such a roller coaster of emotions. What were we doing there? I wanted to take her away, away from all those Souls, somewhere I could remind her that she was mine. Stella dipped her fingers into the black liquid and began to draw marks on my face. "I'm guessing this isn't ink," I said.

"It's black blood, prepared according to an ancient Grimash tradition." Her fingers slid down to my neck, drawing who knew what marks. She was so close our knees were touching. "Your turn," she said, her dark eyes probing inside me.

I dipped my fingers into the black blood and touched them to her face. "Do you remember that 'Stella' means 'star'?" Back during the war, she'd been all I ever thought about. She was my North Star, who would guide me home.

"You always used to ask me that," she said in a soft voice. Sharing old memories with Stella was as painful as it was moving.

"What does 'Kahlena' mean?"

Stella's expression darkened. "'She who has the courage to endure.'"

"Sounds like a perfect name." It couldn't have been easy for her to change and adapt in order to survive, but she had done it.

She watched me steadily as I painted butterfly wings around her eyes, sharp-edged, like her warrior spirit. I traced two marks on her cheeks, hypnotized by her lips. I touched them with my thumb and held it there for a long moment, gripped by a primitive desire to bite them. With the blood I outlined her neck, sliding my fingers down to her breast as our eyes confessed our most hidden secrets.

A shrill whistle broke the bubble of silence in which she and I had sought refuge. I clenched my fists. Vargan was calling for everyone's attention.

"Hey everybody, don't you think this celebration is missing something?"

"Elixir!" they all cried in unison, raising old goblets into the air.

"Full cups is what we want. Elixir's better than hum! Where's the apothecary?" some Soul who must have been from Merry Olde England cried.

Stella shook her head and stood up.

"Where are you going?"

"To get them what they want before a riot breaks out."

I followed her inside the cave to the weapons room, where she took out some containers full of a red liquid. She shook them and poured a little of the liquid into two glasses. Pushing one across the counter, she said, "First taste goes to the guest of honor."

I looked at the red liquid and then at her, amazed. "You're an apothecary."

Stella shrugged. "You pick up lots of things when you're learning to survive. Come on, try it. It's my personal stock. Higher quality."

I grabbed the glass and knocked back the liquid in a single gulp. She stared at me with a little grin on her face and then did the same. There was no doubt about it: she was my soulmate. "You're quite the expert," I said. "It's really good."

"The hell it is! It's more than *good*. It's heaven."

I moved closer to her, one eyebrow raised. "It's also an aphrodisiac."

She smiled and threw back another shot. "So they say."

"Then we should take advantage of it." I pulled her against me and kissed her neck. "Why don't we go make love? Just the two of us," I whispered.

She pulled away from my kisses. "Drake—"

"What's the matter?"

"There are a lot of people out there. Be a good boy, now."

"I don't care about other people, you should know that. After the party we're leaving. I told you I would find a way to get you out of here, and that's what I'm going to do."

"Well, I care."

"About anyone in particular?" I stared at her suspiciously. "You've been with Vargan, haven't you? Has he *touched* you?" Just saying the words sent the blood rushing to my head. "You've been with him. That's why you had his clothes in your house. Tell me the truth."

Stella's expression turned cold. "It's none of your business."

"Yes it is," I shot back, inches from her face. "You're mine, Stella."

"I'm Kahlena. I belong only to myself," she hissed, furious.

"You made love with me."

"It was because of the poison. The steam in the grotto went to our heads."

"No! You can't act like nothing happened. You can't push me away like this. What's happened to you?"

"Hell," she said, serious. She picked up the tray of cups with the Elixir and stormed out. I gripped the countertop as anger flared inside me like a lightning bolt ready to destroy. With a frustrated growl I knocked everything off the counter, sending the weapons crashing to the floor.

Tricu rolled over to my side and looked up at me. "Go away, you stupid mutt." I heard the Souls cheering the arrival of the Elixir and decided I might as well go out there and get drunk.

When I came out of the cave, Stella was standing bare-foot in the middle of the throng, moving her body lithely like a black flame in the middle of a fire. The woman named Ada was with her. When the rhythm changed other Souls joined in, beginning a dance with a medieval beat. Vargan walked over to Stella and offered her his hand, inviting her to dance. Instinctively, her eyes flew to me, but she didn't turn him down. Just the opposite: she used the opportunity to provoke me. The dance grew more sensual and she moved her body together with his, her eyes glued to mine. A Soul was passing me and I ripped the large cup out of his hands.

Unable to take it any more, I walked away from the party and headed toward the river. There was no way I was going to stay there watching a bunch of Souls high on Elixir.

I sat at the water's edge, determined to do what I had been best at doing on Earth. I gulped down a long swig of the warm liquid and felt it gliding down my throat and then surging back up to my head. I'd missed the sensation. "Now we're talking."

Lying back, I contemplated the dark sky. From time to time lightning bolts split it in two. There was no thunder, only luminous streaks that danced to the rhythm of the now-distant music. Part of me couldn't accept what Stella had become. When I'd discovered she was still alive I'd fooled myself into thinking that all I had to do was find her. That part had been unexpectedly easy. But she had changed. I would have to adapt. Finally I had found an opening in her heart—she'd let me find it—but I couldn't expect her to offer it to me. I had to give her more time to get used to me again. To get used to us.

I took another swig of Elixir and stood up, ready to return to her. I couldn't believe that I, of all people, was thinking it, but the party was a waste of time. We had to find a way out of Hell. I would get her out of there or spend eternity trying.

"Drake!" A voice I didn't recognize shouted my name, sounding alarmed. A moment later Ada came running out of the forest.

"I'm right here. Calm down. What's going on?"

"Kahlena!" She was out of breath, but what scared me most was the look in her eye. "They took her."

My world crumbled into a pile of black dust.

10

BATTLEFIELD

"What the fuck? They took her? Who did?!" I shouted, alarmed.

A hiss broke the silence and Ada's head teetered unnaturally on her shoulders. Her black blood splattered my face. "Ada!" I watched in shock as her head slid off her neck. A moment later, her body exploded in a black cloud.

"Draaake!" Stella's frightened scream pierced the night. A shudder made my blood run cold and I leapt into action. I could hear Tricu grunting as I raced desperately toward the clearing, trying to make out other sounds through the ominous silence. At the fire I came to a halt. The party was over. Bodies of the Damned lay on the ground, mutilated or abandoned in puddles of black blood.

"Fuck!" I swore. I searched among the bodies for Stella, moving piles of flesh and bones. "Stella!" I screamed, out of my mind with desperation. Who knew what kind of infernal creature had brought the party to an end in that black bloodbath? Why hadn't Vargan defended her?! There was no trace of him either. Could he be dead?

A grunt interrupted my thoughts. It was Gurdan, lying facedown on the ground. I rushed to him. He wasn't dead. None of those present were, otherwise they would have disintegrated. That was why not finding Stella among the bodies was even more ominous.

The ogre's hand had been chopped off but his fingers were already growing back. "Gurdan, talk to me! What happened?! Where's Stella?"

"Kahlena hit." He gurgled something in his own language that I didn't understand.

"What do you mean 'hit'? Where is she?" I shook him by the shoulders and he put something in my hands. It was my dog tag, the one I'd given Stella . . . and it was covered with black blood.

I couldn't accept that she had disintegrated. Ada had said she'd been taken. "Who did this to you?"

"I did."

The voice turned my body to ice. *Kreeshna*.

I whirled around and the Witch smiled at me, her expression smug. Blind with rage, I strode to her and shoved her against a tree. "Where is she?!" I snarled. "What did you do to her?!"

"I invited her to a much larger party," she said, her expression shrewd.

"You try to hurt her and I'll hunt you down to the very heart of Hell."

The Witch's smile grew even wider. "Sounds amusing."

"Tell me where she is!" I shouted. "Let her go."

The Witch shook her head. "Freedom has its price."

"I'll go with you," I promised. "I'll fight for you."

"Of course you will. You know, your Kahlena did a good job hiding. I might never have tracked her down. But did you really think I wouldn't find *you*? Your soul belongs to me." The Witch touched her Dreide complacently. Each Witch collected in her medallion the purest essence of the Subterraneans she claimed. That was where she had trapped a piece of my soul. The relic lit up, reminding me she was right. The moment I had received the Kiss of Darkness I had become one of her slaves and she had become my Amìsha.

"You led me to her," she went on, "and now she's going to lead you back to me. Your next battlefield is Hell. Good luck, Child of Eve. If we meet again, you'll be my Champion." The Witch disappeared with a sneer on her lips as her voice filled my mind: *Your first challenge begins now.*

With a howl of desperation I smashed my fist into the tree trunk over and over again until my hands were covered with blood. "Stellaaa!!!" My scream shook the forest. Even the most fearsome of the Damned would be smart to steer clear of me.

I climbed the outer rock wall of the cave as lightning bolts lit up the sky overhead. I dragged myself to the top, a height not even the massive trees dared challenge. In the distance, the lightning branched, becoming an electric spiderweb ready to catch me. The Witches generated the lightning, so the Castle had to be right there. If Stella was in their clutches, I was prepared to let myself be captured.

I slid down the rock and grabbed hold of some vines. I had to return to the cave before setting out. Once inside, I collected a bow and arrows, daggers, ropes, and all the other equipment I could carry.

The rock sealing off the door to the cave rumbled aside and a giant walked in, stooping as he crossed the threshold.

"Princess save warrior girl. Gurdan help."

In other circumstances I would have laughed at his clumsy attempt to help me, but I was done joking. "You can't come with me." I looked him up and down. "You're injured."

"Gurdan come." The ogre stepped forward as a sign of his determination.

"The Witches will kill you," I insisted.

"Then Gurdan die."

I looked at him steadily. He showed no signs of fear or hesitation. He came over to the counter and with a single hand picked up half of the weapons in Stella's arsenal. "I carry weapons," he said to convince me.

"All right, then. After all, you could come in handy."

He nodded and together we left the cave. Gurdan sealed off the entrance with the boulder and then followed my gaze, looking up at the sky.

"We'll follow the lightning. It'll lead us to the Castle," I told him. "Hang in there, Stella," I murmured to myself. "I'm coming to get you."

A lightning bolt lit up the sky over our heads, sealing my promise.

STELLA

A REASON FOR EVERYTHING

My first instinct as I came to was to grab my daggers, but they were gone. I opened my eyes and saw the world upside down. I was dangling by my feet and below me Hell was whizzing by. Suddenly it all came back to me. I had been captured by the Witches, and now one of them was taking me somewhere on her Saurus.

I bent double at the waist and touched the rope binding my feet. The poison it was impregnated with instantly burned my fingers. My leather gloves only protected my palms, but I didn't let go. I pulled with all my might, silently hoisting myself up onto the animal's massive back. It was enormous, like a dragon. I had never touched one. Its hide wasn't as tough as it looked.

Freeing myself from the ropes, I flung them over the Saurus's back into the void. The Witch didn't seem to have noticed my movements. Her silver hair streaked with black flowed behind her in the wind. I spotted my daggers in one of the sacks tied to the beast's side and cautiously leaned over. Once I had them in my hands I did a backflip and pointed the blades in the Witch's direction, but she had disappeared. I spun around and she smiled at me craftily.

"Good morning, warrior girl." Her pupils lengthened, as blue as pole stars.

"I'm not impressed." I launched an attack but she skillfully dodged my blows.

She kicked me and I toppled off the Saurus, managing just in time to catch hold of a length of the rope that was still dangling from the animal. Skilled with vines, I swung myself up and landed on top of the Witch. She grabbed me by the legs and flung me onto the animal's back, pointing my own daggers at my throat. I glared at her defiantly.

The Witch smiled. "I wish I could keep playing with you, but we've arrived."

I turned and the Castle loomed up before me, dark and immense. The Saurus reared up and flew to the top of a tower. It landed and the Witch slid off its back. The rope came to life, binding my wrists and jerking me down.

A shiver crept up my legs as I looked around. The tower was the Sauruses' nest, and the giant winged beasts were perched in their stalls. They were majestic, with their black wings. Their mighty claws and barbed tails made them the finest guards anyone could ask for. And they were surrounding us. I looked for a possible means of escape, but could see no way out. Not yet.

The Witch laughed, recalling my attention. "There's a reason you're here. No escape plan could ever work."

My eyes went wide. *The Witch was reading my mind.*

A huge gate opened before us. "That's just one of the little tricks I can do. Want to see another?" All at once I felt myself being slammed into the wall. My back hit the stone so hard it knocked all the air out of me. I tried to move but found I was glued to the wall, my feet not even touching the ground. I looked at the Witch, who hadn't moved an inch. She flashed me a smile and in the blink of an eye was right in front of me. Her blue eyes glimmered as they lengthened like a serpent's while her irises extended over the whites. A hiss made my black blood run ice cold. An actual serpent slithered out from beneath her skin and fixed its hooded eyes on me.

"Be good now," she warned me. "We'll play some more later." She released me from her spell and I fell to the ground. Before I could get up she pulled me along after her. She made her way through the gate and the darkness swallowed us up. "Welcome to your last home. No one leaves the Castle alive."

No. I would never give up hope. And it wasn't true. Drake had managed to escape, after all.

The Witch laughed again, still dragging me behind her. "There's a reason for that too." My mouth fell open when I realized the meaning of what she had just said. Drake hadn't really escaped on his own. The Witches had allowed him to. But why?

The gate closed behind me, sealing me inside.

KAHLENA

Two young women took me by the arms. They wore matching brown combat outfits and each had an intricate tattoo on one arm. They looked strong and highly trained, but they weren't Witches. They were Mizhyas, their slaves. Or, as we called them in the Copse, "she-warriors."

Following the Witch, they led me through various areas of the Castle. Some were well lit and elegant while others were horrifying, full of instruments of torture and cages hanging from the ceiling. I wondered whether they were showing me those on purpose. When we entered a grim-looking stone tunnel I realized we were nearing our destination. The passageway ended in front of a cell. The bars withdrew almost as though afraid of the Witch.

"Let me go!" I struggled to break free of the she-warriors' grip.

"As you wish." The Witch motioned to the two Mizhyas and they shoved me inside.

"Nausyka! You've brought her."

I instantly recognized the new voice and a fire burned inside me. She was the one who had raided the party and slaughtered everyone. It was Kreeshna, the Witch who had subjugated Drake. The same one who had damned me to Hell by seducing me with her promises.

"You were right," Nausyka said. "She's perfect."

I spat at the Witch's feet, my menacing gaze locked on hers. She, however, simply smiled. "I like your temperament. You could be an interesting resource. You just need a little discipline." All at once, leather straps gripped my wrists and ankles, lifting me off the ground.

I screamed in pain as the ropes attached to them pulled taut, threatening to tear me limb from limb. "Let me go!"

Kreeshna came closer, her face inches from mine. "I might, but you'll have to give me something in return."

I frowned. What could she possibly want from me?

The Witch gazed through the bars on the window, which overlooked a courtyard where the Mizhyas were uttering war cries and battling like Amazons. "You'd make a perfect Mizhya. Join us and you'll be free to serve us. What do you say, warrior girl? We repay loyalty very generously."

Her presumption made me snort. "You've got a strange notion of freedom."

"Serving us is a privilege—you'll soon realize that. Until then, enjoy your stay." The Witch turned her back on me and the cell bars slammed shut, trapping me inside. I screamed at the top of my lungs, but the only reply was my own echo.

I hated the Witches because they had damned me to Hell. And now I was their prisoner. They had taken my soul, but I wasn't about to grant them my loyalty. No matter what kind of torture was in store for me, I would never bend to their will. I was Kahlena, warrior of the Grimash tribe.

I looked out the window where the army of she-warriors was now performing a synchronized war march. Hell had forged me. Soon its queens would regret it.

DRAKE

IN THE MIDDLE OF HELL

You led me to her. The Witch's words tormented me as we made our way across a rocky wasteland in search of the Castle. Gurdan was behind me, occasionally letting out grunts.

How had I ever thought I could hide from Kreeshna? I couldn't forgive myself. I'd gone out to find Stella and protect her, but instead I'd put her in danger and now she was in the Witches' hands.

A raven flying overhead cawed as though reproaching me too. Or at least I thought it was a raven. When I saw it alight and hang upside down from a branch I wasn't so sure any more.

What on earth could the Witches want with Stella?

And now she's going to lead you back to me. Kreeshna's voice in my head gave me the answer. It was obvious. The Witch wanted *me*. She wanted me to fight in the Opalion and win the third trial, the one against one of her Sisters' Champions. That way she would win the title of Queen of the Opalion. A fleeting honor, given that the Witches held Games pretty much every other day. Challenges turned them on, inciting constant rivalry among them.

But if Kreeshna wanted me, why abduct Stella? Why not just capture me and throw me into the Arena again? Whatever her reasons, this time I would fight to the death to free Stella, even at the cost of serving those harpies forever. *I had put Stella in danger, and now I had to make things right.*

A sudden noise made me turn around. I went over to the rocks, certain I would find something hidden there, but I was wrong. After one last glance around, I started walking again. We had to be careful. Hell was full of creatures willing to do anything to ensure their next meal, and I had no intention of ending up in the belly of some infernal beast. Not before I'd saved Stella.

Gurdan stopped in his tracks and I almost collided with him.

"What's up?"

"Shh."

He reached out his huge hand, picked up a giant rock from the ground, and studied it closely. Then he sniffed it.

"You hungry, big guy? We don't have time for a snack break."

Gurdan tossed the rock over his shoulder, almost hitting me, then picked up another and started sniffing again. The area around us was full of rocks, so I hoped he didn't mean to smell them all. Before I could figure out what he was doing, he tapped on the one in his hand and started to tickle it. Just when I was about to tell him to stop kidding around, the rock let out a yelp. Seconds later it came to life, unable to resist Gurdan's tickling.

"It's you." I should have known. Stella's stone teddy bear had followed us. "Scram! Go away!"

Gurdan rested him on the ground and shooed him away with his hands. Tricu looked at me and his eyes grew incredibly large, taking on an endearing expression.

I groaned with exasperation. "Oh, do what you want, I don't care. I can't waste any time. We need to get moving." The ogre nodded and walked after me.

I had no idea where the Castle was. We continued to follow the lightning bolts in the sky, hoping they would lead us to Stella, but we never seemed to get anywhere. And yet it couldn't be so far away.

"We've got to climb higher," I said, not waiting for a reply.

We'd skirted a huge rocky mountain, but it was time to climb it. Just as I began to scale the boulders the sound of an explosion made me flinch. I looked down but all I saw was a wave of pebbles that were rolling up the rock as though possessed. I watched them as they passed me and disappeared above us. Tricu let out a grunt from the peak. It was him. Apparently, he not only had the power to summon the rocks around him so he could grow bigger—like I'd seen him do in Stella's cave—but he could break down into smaller pieces too.

Gurdan's foot slipped and he clung to a rocky ledge to avoid falling.

"Hold on tight!" I shouted, going back down to help. Taking out a rope, I tied it around his waist. "Tricu, catch!" I threw it toward the peak. The stone teddy bear caught it in his teeth and struggled to pull the ogre up. Finally Gurdan regained his footing and Tricu released his grip, letting the rope fall down the mountainside.

"No!" I tried to grab it, but lost my balance and felt myself falling backwards. "Shit!" All at once a slab of rock jutted out of the mountainside, breaking my fall. I looked up at Tricu and shot him a gesture of thanks. He let out a yelp. He'd saved my ass. I resumed the climb and finally reached the top, right after Gurdan.

Standing on the summit, I let out a sigh of discouragement. Not even from there could we see the Castle. "Come on. We've got a long way to go." A thump was the only reply. The ogre had plopped down, shaking the ground.

"Gurdan tired."

I groaned. We didn't have time to rest. Tricu rolled over to me. "What do you want? You tired too?" I asked him. He opened his mouth and spat out some prey he'd been hiding inside it. I stared at him, bewildered. "What are you, a hamster?"

Gurdan threw himself onto his back. The long climb had worn him out.

"Oh, all right," I said, giving in. "After all, we do need to eat. Just stay away from me, okay?" I warned the stone teddy bear. He had begun to trot around me as I started a fire.

After eating, Gurdan fell into a deep sleep from which it

was impossible to wake him. *Damn it*. There was no time to lose. Stella might be in danger.

Tricu rolled over to me. He was pretty small now, but I knew he could morph into a boulder in the blink of an eye. "She means a lot to you, doesn't she?" The stone teddy bear gurgled. "I'll take that as a yes. We'll find her," I reassured him. Or maybe I wanted to reassure myself. There was no guarantee Kreeshna would agree to let Stella go even if I won the Opalion for her. Maybe the Witch was just jealous and had already killed her. I bent my knees, pulling my legs in toward me as I ran a hand over my face, banishing the thought.

No. Stella was still alive. She *had to* be. I would never give up, even if it meant turning Hell upside down to find her. Then the Opalion would have a new Champion.

HELL HAS ITS FLAMES

Something tickled my back, waking me from a nightmare. I looked around, suddenly alert. Gurdan was still snoring, while Tricu was standing guard. No one was around, but I could still feel something right beneath me.

When I lifted my legs I saw it: something was burrowing through the ground, raising small ridges of earth that moved quickly in our direction. There were hundreds of them and they had surrounded us. Tricu backed up toward us, growing larger and larger until he was as big as a car.

"Gurdan, wake up." I shook the ogre's shoulder but he didn't respond.

I grabbed my bow and aimed an arrow at one of the ridges, waiting. I had no idea what might be lurking down there. They were like big worms crawling around underground.

Tricu let out a howl that resounded though Hell, even waking up Gurdan. The underground creatures froze. I gripped my weapon, ready to strike. Around the fire, an eerie silence shrouded the twilight. Had Tricu's cry scared them off? At that instant, something burst from the ground and flew toward me. I shot an arrow at the little creature, pinning it to a tree. Was it a ferret? Before I could even figure out what it was, another one emerged from the ground and sank its teeth into my calf. I bellowed in pain and yanked it off me.

Another of the ferrets launched itself at me but I clutched it in midair before it could bite my face. The little beast convulsively chomped its teeth in midair, its eyes crazed with hunger.

"Sorry, we can't stay for dinner." I crushed it in my fist and it squealed before going limp in my hand. Gurdan began to crush them before they could even emerge from the dirt, but there seemed to be an endless stream of them. "What are they?!" I shouted to the ogre.

"Leech furies!" he said. He pounded his massive fist on the ground and crushed one of their heads. The small creature's body stopped moving, its black blood pooling around it. I shot arrows nonstop and when I ran out I moved on to the daggers. A fury clamped its jaws onto the back of my neck and another attached itself to my side. There were too many of them and they were ravenous. Not even Gurdan would be enough to curb their combined hunger. I slammed my back into a tree and cried out when the fury's teeth dug even deeper as it died, then tore the other one off my side and flung it into the fire. The little beast let out a final squeal.

Tricu rammed into the creatures headfirst, sending them flying every which way. A group of furies shot toward me. To dodge them, I dove to the ground in a somersault. I grabbed one that hadn't fully emerged and smashed it into another one. The two furies gnawed on each other in a bath of black blood.

I pulled a stick out of the fire and tried to ward them off with it. It worked, but not enough to keep them entirely at bay. Gurdan searched our cache of weapons. He put something in his mouth and tossed another one to me. They were Stella's strange white stones. It wasn't the time to ask whether they were breath mints. "What do I do with it?"

The ogre picked up another flaming stick and stood behind me, back to back. "Chew and blow." Without hesitating I popped the mint into my mouth. It burst open with a sweet flavor.

A group of at least ten furies leapt toward me all at once. "Blow!" Gurdan shouted. I did, and the flame from the stick burst into a cloud of fire, incinerating the creatures in midair. Behind me, Gurdan did the same. Within seconds we had exterminated them all. He had become a flame-spewing ogre.

I chucked the stick to the ground, studying the demoniacal carbonized bodies all around me. Stella must be an excellent apothecary to have created such a powerful weapon. I tasted the flavor of poison, but evidently she had transformed it into a substance that wasn't lethal for her. I gripped one of the mints in my fist. I had to find her, fast.

Something moved underground, but Gurdan crushed it before it could come out. The last fury.

"Come on. Time to get moving," I said. If that had been our wake-up call, I didn't dare imagine what lay ahead.

WE CROSSED THE STONY EXPANSE, which was covered with rocks as far as the eye could see. Some were twisted into spectacular shapes and emitted dazzling silvery reflections.

Tricu seemed comfortable, unlike us. We had to protect ourselves from the shower of gravel whenever he decided to change size or have a snack. I couldn't have had a weirder traveling companion. I felt like I was trapped in one of the Ubisoft video games I'd spent so many hours playing on Earth as a Subterreanean: a soldier wandering through Hell in search of the castle to which his princess had been abducted. Even the bare tree trunks were buried in rock, as though lime had been poured from the sky to cover them. Their branches stretched upward in an endless cry for help.

Of the Castle, there was still no trace. From time to time I thought I glimpsed it through the spectral mist, but then it vanished. I became convinced it was only a mirage caused by my longing to save Stella. I hadn't saved her from the bullets when she'd been killed on Earth. I hadn't saved her soul when the Witch had come to claim her and take her to Hell. All because I hadn't been there to protect her. But this time I was, and no devil from Hell would keep me from saving her.

"Stop," I ordered. Gurdan and Tricu halted immediately. Before us, a thick network of trees blocked our way.

"Black forest," Gurdan told me.

That wasn't what worried me. I held a finger to my lips and gestured to them with my head. "Down there," I whispered. Two figures could be seen among the trees. They looked small and human, but by now I had learned that they weren't to be trusted, no matter what they were.

We crept closer but the figures didn't move. Their backs were turned to us and at first I thought they were two Souls kneeling down, but the half-light had tricked me. They were two children.

I walked around them to see their faces and cringed. Their bodies were carbonized, their eyes wide open and pitch-black, their pointy teeth frozen in expressions of terror. "Unholy Souls," I murmured.

I knew the only children in Hell weren't really children. The Unholy were those who in life had lost all their faith, choosing to live in evil. Their curse was to age in reverse, that is, grow younger and younger until they disappeared. That was why children were the most feared Souls of all. The younger they were, the more skilled and dangerous they became. Unlike Eden, where Souls had eternal life, it was a constant battle to survive for Souls in Hell, and sooner or later they all died. Though the two Souls in front of us weren't really children, it was still a spine-chilling sight.

I looked around in search of the creature who had reduced them to that state. Whatever it was, it was lethal and it was still out there somewhere. "Let's get out of here."

Before we could move, the ground trembled beneath our

feet. Tricu whimpered nervously and instantly rolled away, urging us to follow him. I peered around, but saw nothing. Then, all at once, I saw a massive black cloud rushing in our direction, bursts of flame glimmering ominously inside it.

"Gurdan, run! What the fuck is that thing?"

"Cinder blizzard. Burn," the ogre said. His footsteps shook the ground as we raced away from the moving bonfire. "You no breathe," he warned me. He was right. The two Unholy Souls had probably been hit by it and been burned to a crisp by its glowing embers.

The blizzard was too close. It scorched my arms and singed my back with millions of tiny flames. We were about to end up trapped in a whirlwind of fire.

The stone teddy bear stopped rolling and whimpered.

"Tricu, don't stop!" He was waiting for us, but unless he kept going the blizzard would catch up to him too. Once I got closer, I realized I was wrong. The ground dead-ended in a sheer cliff and there was nowhere to go. Unless . . .

"This way, quick!" A rope was suspended from one side of the chasm to the other. It was all that remained of an old bridge. "Come on, hurry!" I wasn't sure the rope was strong enough to support all three of us, but we had no choice. The cloud was getting closer and closer.

I tugged on the rope to make sure it was intact. Looking down, I grabbed it with my hands and feet. So high up the bottom couldn't be seen, I was literally hanging by a thread. One hand after the other, I quickly shinned over to the other side, pulling with my arms and dragging my feet behind me.

"Shit!" Gurdan was behind me, but Tricu had remained at the edge of the chasm. "Come on, boy! Find a way to cross——" His squeal of pain made the words catch in my throat as the blizzard swept over him with its incandescent fury. The dust and debris from the fire reached the center of the chasm, lost their impetus, and fell toward the bottom.

When the air cleared, Tricu had vanished.

STELLA

TO THE LAST SHE-WARRIOR

My head shot up when my cell door opened. By now I felt like I'd been there for an eternity. I had always hated the Witches, but during my imprisonment I had learned to hate the Mizhyas even more. One of them in particular: Khetra. She treated me worse than the others did. It was as if she had something against me. Or maybe she was just a bitch.

Luckily she wasn't among the three Mizhyas who burst into the cell. I remembered the names of two of them. The blond one with the tattoo between her breasts was Lenora. Dalitza, on the other hand, had orange hair. It was gathered to one side and braided, accentuating the spotted tattoo on her arm. Not all the Mizhyas were nasty, but the ones who served Kreeshna—and a few of the other Sisters—were the worst.

I held their gaze, my chin held high. I had never, even

for one second, allowed them to believe I was subjugated to them. It would never happen.

Defiantly, I jerked on the chains. Lenora undid the straps around my wrists and I thudded to the floor, my ankles still bound. They were careful not to free me completely. The first time they had freed my legs, leaving me hanging by my wrists. They thought they would have some fun, but I had wrapped my legs around the neck of one of them and smashed her against the wall.

"Come on, Little Miss Insane, time for recess," Dalitza told me.

I struggled as they dragged me out. "I wish I *were* Insane. If I were I would bite your head off in chunks." I had always feared the idea of losing my humanity, and lately I'd come pretty close. And yet just then I really wished I was. When the Mizhya laughed I bit down on her hair and jerked my head back. "Who knows, maybe I'm going insane right now."

She turned around to confront me, her face an inch from my own. "Save your energy for the field, sweetheart."

"The field? Where are you taking me?" The Mizhya turned around with a sneer, dragging me behind her.

Swarms of black butterflies fluttered through the rooms. They were the Souls of the Damned that arrived at the Castle after they died. I knew that well enough, because I had been one of them before being spat out into the Dark Copse.

We crossed through much of the Castle, finally reaching the large courtyard where a massive group of Mizhyas was training. It was the same place they held the Opalion, though during the Games the Arena transformed. At the moment it was nothing but an earthen battlefield.

"Free her," Dalitza ordered Lenora.

I looked around, confused. All the she-warriors had stopped what they were doing and were gathering in a circle around me. "What's going on?" I asked warily.

Dalitza smiled. "I told you, it's recess." I looked at them one by one. They seemed to be preparing to attack me. "You need to choose which side you're on, sweetheart. Or we'll find a way to convince you. You see, we want you to be one of us."

Before Lenora finished freeing my ankles, I wrapped the chain around her neck with a swift movement of my foot and jerked her to the ground. "I'll never be one of you."

Dalitza put herself on guard. "Let's find out why Kreeshna is so interested in you." She attacked me with a high kick but I ducked it and grabbed her foot, then shot to my feet to make her fall, but the Mizhya spun around and freed herself.

"Now I get it! You're jealous because your mistress thinks more of me than she does of you," I said with a sneer, counterattacking.

She laughed, then spat out, "This isn't about you. We hold our own little tournaments, sweetheart."

"What's the prize if I win?"

"Your life."

I snatched the dagger from one of the Mizhyas surrounding us and jammed it into her neck. I had gotten good at the art of stealing, especially when it came to weapons.

"I'm afraid only my own won't be enough," I shot back mockingly. The Mizhya exploded in a cloud of ash and I backflipped away to avoid breathing in the toxic fumes. I would kill them all, down to the very last she-warrior. I would be as deadly as the plague. There would no longer be an army for me to join.

Before I could get the dagger back the Mizhyas attacked me all at once. A fierce battle ensued. I gave it my best, leaping and spinning like I never had before, battling more ferociously than ever, pushing myself to the limit. Hell had taken everything from me, but it had taught me a lot too, especially how to survive.

Black blood splattered my face as I killed the Mizhyas one by one. What for them had begun as a game had turned into a massacre. Now they *really* wanted to annihilate me. If I had to succumb, I would take down as many of them as possible with me. They were the Witches' she-warriors, and for that reason alone they deserved to die.

A blade wounded me, sending a searing pain through my thigh. I turned to see who had done it and found her right in back of me. "Khetra. I was wondering where you were hiding. Joining the party?"

She must have been some sort of general among the she-warriors, because all the others stopped to make way for her. "You mean do I want to teach you a lesson? I can't wait." She smiled as she slashed her sword through the air toward me.

I dodged her attack and got my hands on a staff. It was just the two of us in the center of the Arena, caught up in a deadly dance as the remaining Mizhyas enjoyed the show. It didn't take me long to disarm her. She was good, but I had battled even more ferocious opponents. "What are you, their commander?"

A Mizhya tossed her a staff and the battle resumed. "There are no commanders among us. We're all blood sisters."

"So they follow you just because you're a bitch."

Khetra let out a war cry, attacking me again and again. She struck my staff so hard it snapped in two, then charged me in a rage and pounced on me, pressing my own weapon against my throat. A sneer spread over her face.

"I bet you miss Drake."

My eyes went wide with surprise. What could that Mizhya know about Drake and me?

Khetra neared her lips to my ear. "I miss him too," she whispered. "Especially his hot, sweaty body after a battle. Guess who used to treat his wounds."

Black rage flooded through me. I planted my feet on her chest and hurled her away, then jumped to my feet. Sliding across the dusty ground, I snatched four daggers from the thigh sheaths of two Mizhyas. Khetra seemed surprised by my agility, but she hadn't seen anything yet. She didn't even see it coming. She gasped when I aimed two daggers at her throat and two at the nape of her neck, ready to cut her head off. It would only take a flick of my wrist. I would gladly kill her just because she was a Mizhya, but with her insinuation she had signed her death sentence.

She looked me in the eye. I was astonished to find not a trace of fear on her face. She was prepared to die in the service of her sovereign. I simply couldn't understand why.

"You call yourselves she-warriors, but you're nothing more than slaves. Why are you so hell-bent on serving the Witches?"

"Because this fortress is a good place to live. It's Hell out there."

I smiled. I wasn't afraid of Hell. Not any more. "You're right. Out there it's pure hell. And I am its queen." I tightened my grip on the daggers and prepared to deliver the final blow.

"Enough!" a stern voice boomed, interrupting the battle. All the Mizhyas bowed. Kreeshna walked up to me and smiled. "Let the Mizhya go so she may bow before me."

I didn't deign to look at her. Instead I pressed one of the blades against Khetra's neck. It became tinged with black as blood trickled over it.

Seeing that I wasn't obeying her, the Witch unleashed her power and the blades disintegrated in my hand. I dropped the scorching-hot remains of the daggers.

Free, Khetra bowed to Kreeshna. I, on the other hand, turned to face her.

"Don't you want to pay tribute to me as well?" the Witch asked me tauntingly. Behind her invitation lurked a clear threat. I spat a mouthful of saliva mixed with black blood at her feet. The color of my blood was the same as Khetra's, but I would never subjugate myself to Kreeshna.

To my surprise, the Witch laughed. "I heard what you said. What you think. A cockroach who thinks she's a queen? A little too ambitious, but we can work on that. You would be an excellent addition to my team."

"Kill me if you have to, because I'll never bow before you."

The Witch stared at me intently and suddenly a force raged through my body, filling my head and expanding until it felt as if it would explode. Blood dripped from my nose, black as the darkest magic. My knees buckled and Kreeshna smiled with satisfaction. "Very good. That wasn't so hard, now, was it? If I had wanted to kill you, I would've done it already."

I ran the back of my hand under my nose, wiping away the blood. "Using your tricks is the only way you'll ever force my knee to bend—but you'll never bend my will."

"Don't be so sure about that."

"You tricked me once, when you stole my soul and damned me to Hell. Now I know who you are. I'll never follow you of my own free will. I'll never join you."

"Not even if Drake's life hangs in the balance?" The look of dismay on my face gave her the answer. "Just as I thought." She nodded to her Mizhyas, who picked me up from the ground. I wrenched myself free and they let me go.

"Follow me. There's something I want to show you."

16

THE HEART OF HELL PUMPS BLACK BLOOD

A round table occupied the entire room, which was otherwise bare. The black carbonado walls glimmered in the light of a multitude of small luminous spots in the ceiling. Ironically, they looked like stars. I stopped in my tracks and studied them. I'd forgotten what it felt like to stare up at the sky.

It was weird how the Castle had some rooms that were medieval and others that were futuristic. At least to me they seemed futuristic. I didn't know how Earth had changed since I'd left it.

The massive door closed behind me, sealing us inside.

"What is this place?" I asked cautiously.

"This, my dear, is the heart of Hell. Each Witch has her crystal ball." Upon the Witch's command, the table came to life, becoming a 3-D landscape complete with trees, rocks, and waterfalls.

Fascinated, I moved closer, recognizing some of the places. It looked like a miniature version of Hell. I reached out to touch it and found it wasn't an inanimate scale model, it was live. Within it, creatures moved, escaped, killed; water flowed from the waterfalls and the wind blew through the trees. Everything was moving and changing so quickly I could barely make out the details. It was Kreeshna who was controlling it with her black magic. The Witch seemed to be looking for something.

"What are you doing? Why did you bring me here?" Instead of answering, she gave me a sly smile as everything abruptly came to a halt. A sudden movement caught my eye and I looked up from the model to see a face lighting up one of the walls of the chamber. "Drake . . ." I murmured, my blood running cold. He looked anxious and in danger. "What's going on? What are you doing to him?"

Kreeshna laughed. "I'm not doing anything. Many dangers lurk in the Dark Copse, though. And I can control them." She waved her hand over the table, generating a black fog that trembled with glimmers of fire. Drake looked over his shoulder and started running, along with Gurdan and Tricu. The cloud was chasing them. The whole room had transformed: all the walls had come to life, showing the Copse and its dangers. It wasn't just a projection, though. It all seemed real, as though if I reached out I could touch it. I felt like I was inside the beating heart of Hell.

I followed Drake's escape, turning to track his movements as he passed from one wall to the next, the landscape transforming before him. He came to a sudden halt at the brink of a cliff and almost fell off the edge.

"Drake!" I screamed, but the illusion faded and the walls went dark. Furious, I turned toward the Witch. I wished I could suffocate *her* in that cloud of fire and forever deform that sinister smile of hers. "What happened to him?" I asked, frantic.

"He's out looking for you, poor thing. He doesn't realize that Hell is an ever-changing place. It might take him centuries to find his way back to the Castle." The miniature on the table showed the dark fortress, but it vanished instantly, reappearing in another spot. "I'll ask you again: are you ready to join the Mizhyas?"

If hatred was a fire I would have turned to ash. Damn it, Drake! Sooner or later I would have found a way to escape. Why was he coming to find me? Kreeshna wouldn't make things easy for him, that was for sure.

"It can't be fun, wandering around looking for someone for all eternity—especially when you're being hunted." On the enchanted table, a huge beast crept out of a lake. It was black, mighty, with sharp fangs and claws. A cross between a feline and a bear. Drake reappeared on the wall and, at a wave of the Witch's hand, the feline bounded into the tree above him.

"Look out!" I cried, leaning toward the screen. But Drake couldn't see or hear me. There was nothing I could do to help him.

"After all, it seems like a fitting punishment for abandoning me. To each his own fate. Maybe I should take back my offer and leave things as they are. It's more fun this way." Just then, the beast split into two separate beasts. I raised my eyes and glared at Kreeshna. She smiled, reading my surrender in my mind. All at once a group of Mizhyas ran into the room and surrounded me. "May the blood ceremony begin," the Witch proclaimed. "Don't worry, it's nothing formal."

Khetra held a bracelet close to my bicep. At a gesture from the Witch, it burst into flame, illuminating the carved symbols on it.

"Welcome to the she-warriors."

The Mizhya clamped the metal around my arm and the searing pain blinded me.

DRAKE

17

A PRICE TO PAY

G urdan tore the creature off me, smashing it against the rock, but another one was lying in wait and attacked the ogre from behind. It looked like a Yeti of darkness and was even bigger than he was.

"Gurdan, move aside!"

When he saw the drawn bow in my hand he threw himself to the ground. I shot two arrows at the same time, but halfway to their target they hit an invisible wall and vanished, generating a blast of energy that sent me crashing back against a tree.

Suddenly everything went quiet. I looked around, disoriented. The beasts had disintegrated and there was no sign of Gurdan either. But something even more surreal had happened: the black Castle now stood before me, majestic and terrifying. At last I had found it, and inside it was Stella. A shiver ran through me. It was as vast as I remembered, but even more foreboding. Something told me that once I went inside I would never leave again.

The gates opened and a small procession of Mizhyas marched toward me. Khetra headed the group, which told me Kreeshna had sent them. There was something different in the Mizhya's face, a malicious indifference I wasn't prepared for. She wasn't my ally, I reminded myself.

"It's rare for an escaped Subterranean to deliver himself to the Castle of his own volition."

"I had a good reason to come back," I said. *The same one I escaped for.*

Khetra snorted, but her expression betrayed her. She was jealous. "You had your freedom. It would've been wiser to hold on to it."

"I've never really been free." *Not since I lost Stella on Earth.*

"Well, now you've lost all hope. Once you enter the Castle, I doubt you'll ever get out again."

Was it possible she was suggesting I turn back? Maybe she was trying to make me leave in order to separate me from Stella. If so, she was kidding herself. I would never give her up. Not without a fight.

"Take me to Kreeshna," I told her, resolute.

Khetra stepped behind me and bound my hands behind my back. "Your mistress is already expecting you," she whispered in my ear. She just couldn't pass up the chance to remind me I was a slave there.

Two Mizhyas escorted me into the Castle and up to a large wooden door. They unbound my hands and turned to stand guard. I imagined Kreeshna was inside, so I reached out to turn the knob, but the door swung open on its own, welcoming me into the large room.

When I stepped inside, Stella's eyes instantly found mine. "Drake!" She rushed toward me and I darted forward, but Kreeshna snapped her short-handled, five-tailed whip and yanked Stella back.

"Let her go!" I snarled at the Witch. Stella had barely touched me, and being deprived of that contact burned my chest. I wanted to embrace her, feel that I had found her again, that she was mine.

The Witch smiled, reading the desire in my mind. "Why should I? She's mine now," she replied with a sneer.

It was then that I saw it: the tattoo on Stella's arm, an armband just below the elbow that branched down her forearm. She had become a Mizhya. She was one of them.

"What's going on?" Only now did I realize that she looked just like the rest of Kreeshna's she-warriors: she was wearing the same brown combat outfit. She even emanated the spirit of a she-warrior—it had always been inside her. "Stella, *why*?"

Her distressed expression left room for hope that she hadn't done it by choice. "They forced me," she confirmed, desperation in her tone.

Kreeshna snorted. "Don't lie. You chose freely."

"She kept sending out beasts to hunt you down," she said. "I *had* to do it."

"No, you didn't!" I said reproachfully. I glanced at the large table that occupied almost the whole room, where a miniature version of Hell was crawling with familiar creatures and settings. So that was how things worked. I had never actually been free of Kreeshna. She had continued to manipulate my choices, *our* choices, abducting Stella to make me return to her and then forcing her to swear an oath of loyalty. She had stolen her from me. It had always been that way between the Subterraneans and the Witches: a battle over Souls. It was as though we were still back on Earth. They couldn't resist demonstrating their superiority over us. Now Stella would have to obey Kreeshna's every command. What was that harpy scheming? Even worse, what would it mean for us?

"Why did you leave me out there?! Why didn't you take *me*?"

Kreeshna gave no answer. At her command, Stella was dragged out of the room. She struggled to prevent it but could do nothing.

"Drake!"

"Stellaaa! Let her go! What do you want from her?" I growled at the Witch. The Mizhyas held me back, preventing me from attacking her.

"You can still have her, under my conditions. If you refuse, she'll be mine forever."

"You would've shown me the way back to the Castle anyway, wouldn't you? You lied."

"The truth is so boring. You can achieve so much more by using a touch of imagination."

I shot Kreeshna a fiery glare. "I'm here now, just like you wanted. Ready to challenge everything and everyone." I would do anything to free Stella. I would do battle in the Opalion and emerge victorious for Kreeshna.

The Witch read my mind before I could even make my

offer. She smiled. "Poor fool, do you still not understand? *I* orchestrated your escape. I *decided* to allow you to run away from the Castle. One doesn't become a Champion so easily. Each Subterranean needs to earn the privilege of being chosen. While you were out there believing you'd embarked on a journey to save your beloved, I was actually training you so you'd be worthy. But winning the Opalion isn't enough to make me spare both your lives. It certainly wouldn't be worth losing the strongest Champion I've ever trained. Do you really believe I've done all this for a stupid Opalion? Freedom has a far higher price."

"What do you want, then?"

"I want more. I want glory, glory over all my Sisters. For centuries I've searched for a worthy Champion. I've had many, but none that rose to the level of my standards. You were raw, but I saw your potential right from the start, even when you were nothing more than a mortal enlisted in the army. When I claimed you, you were only a Soldier. Now you've advanced to Champion and soon you'll prove it to everyone. I've seen your skills in battle, without your even having fed on lymphe. Imagine what you could do with my power inside you. The battles in the Opalion trained you, but they weren't enough."

"So you made me believe you were hunting Stella so I would go out and find her to protect her, when you actually never had any intention of tossing her into the Arena to make me demonstrate my loyalty to you. Do I have it right now?"

"There's no such thing as blind loyalty. If you want to trust someone, you need to find a way for their interests to coincide with your own. I wanted you to win for me, and you needed a stronger motivation. Hell forged you, and the woman you love lit your fire. At long last, you're ready."

"Ready for what?"

"The Dark Tournament."

I recoiled at the words. The Ultimate Opalion. Among the Damned and Subterraneans it was a legend mentioned only in whispers.

The Witch nodded. "You'll undergo the most grueling of challenges as you complete each level of the Games and reach the next. It is a contest like few others, in which imagination and reality come together to create a unique battlefield. Among the Damned it's the stuff of legend. They come from all over the realm to witness the event. The Dark Tournament is held once every thousand years and at last the time has come. Unlike the Opalion, you will challenge not one but all of my Sisters' Champions. And finally you too will be one of them."

From what she was saying, there was no choice: I would have to be one. While in an ordinary Opalion the Witches pitted anyone they wanted against their Champion, even prisoners, the Ultimate Opalion was waged only among Champions.

"I've never even won a regular Opalion. What makes you think I'll make it through the trials?"

"You'll do so because the stakes have changed. At each level you'll be convinced you can't do it. My Sisters will make you believe you can't. They'll do whatever they can to obstruct you. But you'll resist, you'll fight for me, you'll destroy for me. You'll win for me. Only then will I become the Queen of the Dark Tournament. And only then will both your lives be spared."

"What if I lose?" I was prepared to sacrifice myself and battle anyone if it meant saving Stella, but up to now I had never won even a single Opalion. She knew that.

"You will give me the glory I deserve," she said, "or you both will die."

I clenched my fists. The very thought of battling all the Witches' Champions was insane. But I could do it. Kreeshna was right, this time it was different. This time, Stella was the prize.

"I accept," I said, determined.

Stella had ended up in Hell trying to follow me. It was my turn to save her.

Even if I died in the attempt.

FREEDOM IS THE COLOR OF BLOOD

The Mizhyas dragged me away from Kreeshna. I was sure they were going to imprison me but instead they took me to the Spa Parlor, a place reserved for the Witches and their Champions. Everything was dazzling inside its grottos. Water emerged in sparkling little cascades from the ceiling and walls, flowing into pools. Some shimmered as though filled with molten gold.

On the way there I'd noticed that the whole Castle was abuzz with Mizhyas and Subterraneans. The stands of the Arena were packed with the Damned, who had come to witness the ultimate tournament. The time had come.

Their murmuring, though, was hushed by the walls of the Spa. We hadn't used doors to enter. Instead, we'd crossed through an invisible wall. It was as though the Spa was in another dimension, a place hidden from the rest of the inhabitants of the Castle. It was like a meditation area.

Rumor had it that the water there was capable of instilling power, but it was a lie. The Witches' blood was our promise of power. With their Dreide they captured our strength. With their lymphe they also claimed our minds. We were granted only one dose, shortly before the Tournament. It would increase our abilities, sharpen our senses, allow the Witches to enter our minds and control us like pawns. Actually, we Champions weren't really the ones battling; it was the Witches. Each of them, as she watched, did everything she could to make her Champion advance a level or destroy his opponents. The real challenge was among the Sisterhood. Only she who demonstrated the shrewdest strategy was worthy of glory.

For us Champions unleashed in the Arena, it was a game of strength and survival, whereas for the Witches, it was a chess match in which only the Black Queen would remain standing. It was clear why Kreeshna had put so much effort into it. Ordinary Opalions were common events and the glory derived from each vanished as soon as the following one was held. What's more, in those tournaments only two Sisters contended for the title. Battling all of them in a challenge that took place only once every thousand years was a lot more important.

The grottos were teeming with Champions. They were all there, being carefully attended to by Mizhyas and their Amìshas. Some were having wax poured over them that would solidify on their bodies, others were being wrapped with red seaweed, while still others were totally immersed in the waters. I wondered if I would have to undergo those treatments too.

Kreeshna's Mizhyas stripped me naked and pushed me into one of the pools. I could see for myself now that it wasn't water, but rather, a golden liquid that glimmered in the torchlight flickering on the walls.

"Where's Stella? Why isn't she here too?" I asked Khetra. "She's one of you now. I want her to be the one to help me."

The Mizhya's gaze turned fiery. "What you want matters nothing here."

Why was she acting like that? She'd never really cared about me and I'd never promised her anything. We'd had fun together, but that was it. That had always been clear to both of us.

Then I understood. Khetra wasn't bothered by the fact that I had only been having fun with her. She was hurt that I didn't feel the same way about Stella. Khetra had known me as a player who didn't take relationships seriously. And I really had become one after losing Stella. For decades I'd vented my suffering in meaningless flings without ever making a serious commitment. Maybe Khetra couldn't stand that Stella had been the one to change me, not her. I'd had lots of women, enough to know how to interpret the way the Mizhya was looking at me.

I didn't care about her jealousy. I wasn't a knight in shining armor. I wanted Stella, wanted her there with me . . . at least to say goodbye to her before the tournament. I grabbed Khetra's wrist. "I'm asking you, where is Stella?"

"Kahlena is at Kreeshna's side. She still needs discipline. Our mistress will find a way to make her more *servile*."

Hearing that name again made my blood boil. It was the

name Stella had insisted on being called when I thought I'd lost her. And now, using that same name, they hoped to take her away from me.

I clenched my fists, desperate at the thought that I wouldn't see her again before the tournament. Before walking into the lions' den.

"You should be pleased," Khetra went on, pouring some of the golden liquid onto my back. "She's going to dance for you during the opening ceremony. She'll be in the front row when they begin the Games, right next to the Black Queen."

I frowned. That should have been good news, but Khetra's sly smirk made me think it actually wasn't. "If you want to flaunt your submission to Kreeshna, just call her 'mistress.' She's not the Queen of the Tournament yet."

"It'll be better for you if she is soon."

I wondered how Sophìa, the Empress and ruler of the kingdom, could allow her Sisters the opportunity to boast such a title. When the Games were over, she was still the queen over all. And yet each of the Witches yearned for that glory. It was a victory over the others. As I thought about it, I realized it must have been Sophìa's strategy to keep them contented and in their place.

Kreeshna made her entrance into the grottos, a small army of Mizhyas following her. I started when I saw Stella among them. Our eyes met but she stayed in her place. I didn't dare imagine what kind of compromises the Witch had forced her into to get her to submit. And now Kreeshna was using her to get me to behave. Stella was a warrior, more courageous than all the she-warriors in the room, maybe in the whole Castle. No one could take that away from her.

Stella was ordered to step forward and undress Kreeshna. What an insult, making Stella deliver her own boyfriend to her. I cast her a regretful glance as the Witch joined me in the pool.

At an order from Kreeshna, the other Mizhyas left the grottos. All of them except Stella. When the Witch disappeared beneath the golden surface it was as though Stella and I were alone in that room full of enemies, our gazes bound to each other as our bodies were frozen in that moment. So close and yet so out of reach.

The surface rippled and Kreeshna emerged, her face like a golden mask. She moved closer to me. The gold glimmered as it trickled down her chocolate-colored skin. She rested her golden breasts against my chest and her magnetic gaze hypnotized me.

The Witch smiled. "I've waited for you for centuries, my worthy Champion."

I balled my hands into fists, my muscles quivering with rage at the thought that Stella was there, that the Witch was forcing her to watch us. I stared at Stella, ignoring Kreeshna's hands as they caressed me. Stella's eyes were aflame, haunted by a touch of sadness she couldn't hold back.

The hiss of a serpent seemed to slow time and all at once I found myself hopelessly attracted to Kreeshna, overpowered by a dark spell I couldn't resist. The Witch bit her lip and a crimson droplet slid down her chin and into the air, splashing onto the golden surface.

Kreeshna brought her face close to mine and it was as

though I had never desired anything else in my whole life. Suddenly I craved her blood, wanted it inside me. I moved my lips closer and my tongue obeyed that summons, touching the scarlet liquid. An explosion set my brain on fire, canceling every thought other than Kreeshna, my queen. It was for her that I had to fight, for her that I had to win . . . or die. I drew her to me and our tongues met, kindling my desire. Her lips throbbed, inviting me to take more. I sucked her lymphe, losing all control as the bewitching liquid went to my head like the most powerful of poisons.

Kreeshna's voice filled my mind. The Witch was already inside me. *My strength will be your strength. Receive my blood within you and let it guide you in battle.* Gahl sum keht. *Forge your glory, my Champion. Make me the Black Queen or die for me.* She was speaking in Kahatmunì, the Witches' ancient tongue, but now I was able to understand it.

"*Kaahmì,*" I replied, without even realizing it. *I am at your command.*

The Witch pulled away and stepped out of the golden liquid, loosening her grip on my mind. When I looked up, Stella was there, her once-proud face now devastated. *She had seen everything.*

Thick golden droplets slid down Kreeshna's body, returning to the pool. She stood there, her back to me, completely naked, as a maidservant who had come unobtrusively into the room draped a black mantle over her.

On Earth I had been a Reaper Angel. Down here I was a prisoner. The Witch tilted her head, a cunning smile on her lips, proud of her first victory. She had triumphed over Stella and me.

19

THE DARK CEREMONY

The disappointment I'd seen in Stella's eyes was killing me. Didn't she know I had been out of my mind? Kreeshna's blood had bewitched me. Its very scent had captivated my every thought, leaving me her prisoner. It was a spell, a lie. True power was the connection between me and Stella. Even Kreeshna knew that. All it took was meeting Stella's eyes to remember what I was fighting for. Her heartbroken expression had wiped away every trace of Kreeshna from my mind.

For a second Kahlena, the warrior, had let her armor fall away, showing me the real Stella, the one who still loved me. Kreeshna wanted to break the bond between us, but I wasn't going to let her. I would do battle for the Witch, but my only queen would be Stella.

At a certain point all the Witches left the Spa and the Mizhyas positioned me, completely naked, in front of a wall.

I glanced to my left where not far away stood another
Champion. I could see two or three of them, standing in the
same position as me, but then the wall curved, hiding the
others further along the circle. The wall trembled and it felt
as though we were ascending, like in an elevator, but actually we weren't moving—it was the Castle that was moving
around us. Within seconds other walls had descended, separating us. I found myself inside a room before a massive
door. Looking around, I saw it was a gymnasium, one of the
several located around the Arena. Each of the Champions
must have ended up in his own.

Something tickled my skin. I stared at my hands as
armor formed over me. The veins in my arms bulged as
black carbonado covered them like a three-dimensional
tattoo. The horn blew and the huge door opened onto
the Arena.

The audience burst into cheers as all nine Champions
made their entrance onto the battlefield, each emerging
from his own door: muscles ready, skin oiled, and black
armor glittering, just like me. Unlike the Opalion, in which
we battled barefoot and shirtless, for the Dark Tournament
we were granted greater protection. My arms were sheathed
from wrists to elbows, leaving my upper arms bare, and a
breastplate protected my chest. My thighs were covered, and
a sturdy black cup protected my package. We were all the
same, like perfect toy soldiers. Each of us wore a long black
mantle and our faces were hidden behind masks of black
and silver jewels fused together with metal spikes. I scruti-
nized my opponents. Only one of us would be left standing.
And it had to be me.

I clenched my fists and scanned the stands for Stella, but didn't see her.

The Arena was a perfect amphitheater. In the stands were the Damned, Souls of every kind, who had no doubt been placing bets. When the horn blew a second time, everyone fell silent and sat down. The sound of drumbeats filled the silence like the beating of a thousand hearts. From a hidden area, a small group of Mizhyas made their entrance into the Arena. Other instruments joined the macabre orchestra and the she-warriors began to perform a tribal dance. I couldn't see whether Stella was among them. Their faces were painted black. They moved as swiftly as panthers, alternating battle moves and perfectly coordinated dance steps. Dark wraiths swirled around them or blocked their way, maneuvered by the Witches' black magic. The spectators clapped to the rhythm of the drums, excited by the dance, which promised sex and death. The music grew louder and louder, the drumbeats faster and faster. I realized there were nine Mizhyas in all, just like us, and that they were enacting a theatrical performance of the Tournament.

The sound suddenly stopped and all the Mizhyas fell to the ground. All except one.

It was then that I recognized her, right there in the center. The only Mizhya still standing. Her eyes found mine across the Arena, penetrating the mask I wore. Not being able to touch her was excruciating, but even more painful was the disappointment I still saw in her eyes that now glared at me bitterly, burning like a sword stabbing me full in the chest. Didn't she know I was prepared to die for her?

Our gazes remained locked until the symbol of the

Witches caught fire all around her. The flames rose and everyone looked up. The sound of thunder joined the drumbeats as the Witches rode into the Arena on their winged steeds.

The Sauruses flew in a circle, spurred on by an ominous war cry. They landed in the center of the Arena, encircling the Mizhyas. A massive throng of butterflies darkened the sky and swooped straight down toward the Witches, splitting into separate swarms. Within seconds, each swarm had arranged itself into the shape of a magnificent chariot for each of the Witches. As the Sauruses reared up, the crowds rose to their feet to applaud the spectacle they had just witnessed.

Each steed marched toward one of the Champions, pulling its chariot behind. Kreeshna had a regal air as she headed toward me, her cat's eyes piercing the night. She wore a helmet and a steampunk gown that made her look both sexy and regal. For the first time, she really did seem like a Black Queen. All of them did . . . and all laid claim to the title.

She stopped her Saurus beside me and her voice filled my head. *"It's time for you to rise above the rest, Champion. Prove you're worthy and you'll have what you deserve."* I climbed into the chariot and she smiled at me. The devil's smile.

Once all the Champions were in their vehicles, the Sauruses marched around the Arena.

I didn't know which was worse: the Witches showing off their Champions, flaunting us to the crowds like trophies, or the bloodthirsty Damned who couldn't wait to witness our massacre. I would have killed them all if

Kreeshna had only asked me to. I would battle for myself and for Stella.

I tried to spot her but she wasn't on the central platform any more. In its place, the dais of honor had appeared and on it was Sophìa, the Empress of the Underworld. It came as no surprise to me that she wasn't taking part in the Games. I was more and more convinced that this was all a ploy to give the rest of her Sisterhood the illusion of power. She was the devil incarnate, after all. Why should she care about a title earned in a tournament? Competition among the Sisterhood, on the other hand, was always fierce. And Sophìa stoked it. The Tournament was proof of that, given that she would allow one of them to call herself "queen."

It was pathetic.

Besides, someone had to arbitrate the match, especially when the people competing against each other were unscrupulous harpies. The Dark Tournament had its rules, though. Each Witch could enhance her Champion's strength with the lymphe she granted him. However, she couldn't help him accomplish his tasks. Not directly, at least. Each of them could hinder her Champion's adversaries, though, giving her own Champion an advantage.

The Witches never missed a chance to show us they were the ones controlling the Games. I'd imagined they would make us guide their steeds while they enjoyed the presentation from their chariots, letting themselves be paraded around like goddesses, but I was wrong.

"My beloved Damned," the Empress began. The Sauruses halted, shoulder to shoulder, and the entire crowd rose to their feet before Sophìa. The Witches descended

from their steeds. "Many of you have come to watch the
Opalion Games for centuries, but that is not why we are
here today." The Empress was speaking in an ancient
dialect. Some might not even have understood her, but they
were all mesmerized by her dark allure. Sophìa was lethal,
and everything about her made that clear, from her piercing
lapis lazuli gaze to the tiny black diamonds adorning the
silver tips of her pointy headdress. Not to mention the small
black serpent coiled around her forearm that hissed with
every word. "Today," she went on, "we are here to celebrate
a special event that takes place but once every thousand
years."

"I seen me a Dark Tournament once before!" someone
cried from the crowd. Another small group called out, vying
for the Empress's attention. Some Souls had been in Hell for
so long they had already witnessed the rare event. The Soul
who had interrupted Sophìa screamed and doubled over,
afflicted by unspeakable pain. He raised a beseeching hand
and his eyes bulged out of their orbits before he burst into a
cloud of ash. The crowd froze and no one dared make
another sound.

The Empress smiled and took a step forward. "Once
was enough for him." The crowds laughed obediently. "May
the Sisterhood present the Champions who will compete in
the Dark Tournament!" The chariots beneath us exploded
into a massive swarm again, carrying us to the Witches'
sides. Then the butterflies flew toward the Empress. They
danced around her as she delighted in the sight of them. At
the Castle, Sophìa was known for her obsession with her
black butterflies. When she disappeared for long periods of

time, she would inevitably be in her garden of Devil's Stramonium, the black flower the Witches fed their Dakor. It was there, they said, that she sorted through the souls of the Damned, assigning them their fitting punishment before spitting them out into Hell.

Something emerged from the ground: black thrones positioned at equal intervals around the Arena.

All ten of the Witches were present at the Games, but Sophìa was the only one not taking part with her own Champion. Actually, since I'd been there I'd never seen him fight in an Opalion. The events he competed in must be few and far between.

The tallest of the Witches presented her contender. Her image was projected onto a temporary screen in the center of the Arena, like a giant hologram. She was beautiful, with light brown skin, golden eyes, and a long ponytail as black as ebony. "My name is Bathsheeva. For the Dark Tournament I offer my Champion: Amihr." His mantle burst into a swirl of butterflies and his mask dissolved, revealing his face. He too had dark skin, bulging muscles, and the look of someone prepared to kill. The audience applauded as he accompanied her to one of the thrones where he bowed at her feet in a final display of subjugation.

The Witches thought they were goddesses. I hated humoring them in their belief.

"I am Anya," said the Witch with brown hair and green eyes. "The warrior Faustian will battle for me." The mask vanished and the face of my friend Faust appeared.

Shit. I was sorry to have to fight against him. I would have no choice but to kill him.

"Camelia is my name." When she stepped forward, the next Witch's hair changed from pink to blue. "Cheer for my Champion, Misha." The crowd did so, excited by the sight of the huge Russian, or maybe impressed by his mistress's little trick. They were doubtless betting on him.

Each Witch came forward in turn and then went to sit on her throne.

It was Kreeshna's turn. I raised one hand, my palm turned upward to receive hers, and walked her to her place, almost stopping in my tracks when I saw Stella beside the throne. As I watched, a helmet formed over Kreeshna's head. It wasn't an actual helmet, since it didn't cover her whole skull; it looked more like a pair of high-tech earphones. It was easy to guess what they were for: to isolate the thoughts of each Witch from those of her Sisters so they wouldn't be able to spy on each other's minds and discover their next moves. The earphones were connected by a butterfly-shaped diadem at the brow. The devices emanated a light and, seconds later, projected a hologram of the Arena onto the Witches' laps. That would probably let them follow our moves from close up and control the Game, blending reality and illusion. I had seen something like it in the room where the Mizhyas had taken me to Kreeshna.

I glanced at the other Witches. Their eyes had also lit up and lengthened into slits, revealing the Dakor lurking within them. I noticed that none of them had a Mizhya at their side. Their she-warriors were lined up behind the thrones. Kreeshna definitely wanted to remind me of what I was fighting for. She didn't want me to lose sight of my *motivation*, as she would call it. She herself cared only about the crown, as black as her heart of stone.

She was right: I had never really cared about winning an Opalion. Now, though, I couldn't afford to lose. Even if it meant subjecting myself to their treacherous rules. Like the others before me, I kissed the back of her hand but didn't deign even to look the Witch in the face. Instead, my eyes burned into Stella's. She turned away, denying me that last farewell. I hated that her last memory of me was my kiss with Kreeshna. I didn't want her to hate *me* for that accursed kiss.

Shouts and cheers distracted me from my thoughts as the last Witch presented her Champion. It was Devina, Sophìa's Specter, second only to the devil herself. Everyone at the Castle feared her, maybe even her Sisters. Her red hair pierced the twilight, her amber eyes were like fire. "I am Devina, Specter of the Empress. Hail, one and all, the Champion who will battle for me: Assin!" The man's mask disappeared and my blood ran cold when I recognized him. His face was branded on my brain like an indelible mark. It was him, the bastard who had sent me to Hell. I clenched my fists at my sides when our eyes met and he smiled. Soon enough I would shove that smirk down his throat.

The Empress spread her hands. Upon her command, a cluster of butterflies formed themselves into a black crown on her palms, its points as sharp as the tips of a black diamond.

"Applaud the nine Champions who will challenge each other in the Dark Tournament. They are exceptional warriors one and all, selected and trained to excel in the arts of battle. Today they will be called upon to demonstrate the finest qualities required of a soldier. Only the most valiant will overcome the trials. They will brave three levels of grueling challenges in order to fight in the final round. In the first level they must accomplish various missions in order to qualify for the subsequent levels. Only six will advance to the second level, which will consist of hand-to-hand combat among the Champions who have qualified. They will be divided into two teams according to their scores. The two Champions who remain will fight to the death. There is a reason it is called the Dark Tournament. Unlike the Opalion, in which our Champions do not truly risk their lives, in this Tournament the Witches who reach the final round will risk everything, since only one of the final two Champions will succeed. The other will be cast into Oblivion, eternal death."

Hearing this, the entire audience let out a cry of dismay. It was common knowledge that the Subterraneans couldn't die. Only Oblivion could undermine their immortality and annihilate them forever.

"It is a pity that one of the strongest and most courageous, one who has come so close to the ultimate victory, must die," the Empress went on, "but these are the things one does for glory. At times our deepest desires are also our downfall, is it not so?" The audience laughed, careful not to anger the Empress. "No Witch is allowed to help her Champion directly, but each may interact with the Arena, creating physical or mental traps and obstacles to hinder the other competitors."

I snorted. In any other tournament it would be seen as

unfair to throw a wrench into the works while battling your opponents, but here it was not only allowed, it was one of the rules.

"The warriors will face each other with courage, intelligence, and strength. They must overcome their fear, use their cunning to survive, be swift to escape dangers, strong to defeat the others. They must endure hostile environments while their senses are put to the test. They must know how to turn off their emotions. They must prove they are worthy. Only the most valiant will win the crown, bringing honor to his queen and thus saving his own life. Each of them has received intensive training at the hands of the Sisterhood, who long for victory as much as their Champions. The Witch who wins the crown will have a thousand years of glory over her Sisters. To us this is worth more than a thousand lives. Competition is everything. May the Dark Tournament begin! *Gahl sum keht.* Forge your glory."

The Empress blew on the crown in her hands and it disintegrated like ash in the wind. Her message was clear: the crown would exist only for the new queen.

I clenched my fists and turned toward the Arena, as did my adversaries. I hated that Witch for everything she had stolen from me. I hated that kingdom. I hated all of them. There was only one way out: to fight.

20

CHARACTER BUILDING

The ground trembled as the horn announced the beginning of the Games. I watched the landscape around me transform. The central hologram had disappeared the second the Empress destroyed the crown. The Witches' thrones rose up, each of them high on a platform that extended over the Arena. Metal spokes stretched out from Sophìa's central throne and connected to each of the others. From where I was standing below them, it looked like a wheel on a macabre funeral cart.

As though wanting to follow the Witches, thick walls emerged from the ground, making the stands and everything else in the Arena shudder. They rose up all around the battlefield, sealing us inside a cylindrical area. Confused, I frowned and tried to figure out what Sophìa, the Stage Director, had in mind.

The tall walls hid us from the Damned. Wasn't it supposed to be a show put on for them? I saw my image filling an entire wall and finally understood: they weren't walls, but rather, screens on which the Games would be projected for the crowds. The scenario the Stage Director planned to create was probably so lethal she couldn't let them take part, not even as spectators.

I turned toward Stella and our eyes met one last time before a tall wall rose up between us, separating us, possibly forever. I felt a pang in my chest and longed to run to her, but it was too late. I was trapped with eight other Champions, all ready to destroy each other.

The Empress appeared on all the screens, followed one by one by each of the Champions alongside his Amìsha. In the background, the drums continued their dark melody. Charts projected on the screens showed the viewers our names, our skills, and who we were fighting for.

I had no idea what had driven the other Champions to this point. Each of them must have trained with their Witch in preparation for the Games. Some had been in Hell for centuries and might have already taken part in a previous Dark Tournament. Maybe some were so devoted that they were fighting just to bring glory to their queen. Others were probably fighting for their lives or their freedom. I was fighting for love, the only love I'd ever known. A love that had followed me even after death, never fading, even though I'd been sure I'd lost her. My eyes stung and I squeezed them shut. Stella had been torn away from me too soon and I wasn't willing to give up now that I had found her again. It was time for me to get her back.

Outside the walls, the crowd whistled as pictures of our training were projected on the screen. This was followed by images of us, one by one, in the Arena, muscles taut and prepared to face any challenge the Witches had in store for us. Was Stella watching me? I didn't want her to see me die.

The shouts became deafening when our faces disappeared and were replaced by another image. Something dazzling. It looked like a laboratory and it came closer and closer, as if the walls were moving in our direction to crush us. We backed up until our shoulders were pressed against the wall, but the light continued to advance, blinding us. Was this how they wanted to kill us off? By crushing us between the Arena walls? It was too late for an answer. I braced for impact . . . but the wall passed right through me.

Looking around, confused, I squinted my eyes against the glaring light. The Arena had disappeared. The cries from the crowd had stopped the second the scenario had sucked us in, and now I found myself in a laboratory, surrounded by decomposing corpses. It was like being in a different world, but I knew where I was: it was an interactive illusion, a manipulation of reality, a virtual game the Witches had created just for us, and we were the avatars.

Even my adversaries had disappeared. We didn't have to face each other in a player-versus-player battle. Not yet. We had to accomplish individual missions in order to level up. Only then would we battle each other. Until that moment, each of us was fighting in his own virtual reality. Like me, the others had their own games to play.

I had been inside scenarios created by a Witch before, so I knew everything was real, not a simple optical illusion. It was black magic. It was our prison. I would have bet my balls they were still there watching us from above, perched on their diamond thrones like vultures, eager to know who would perish first. With their holograms, they would be keeping an eye on the progress of each competitor, never losing track of who was where. Even more importantly, they would be manipulating reality to put the rest of us at a disadvantage so their own Champion could level up. In this tournament, I didn't merely need to face difficulties, like in the Opalion. I would have to overcome them faster than the others. I would have to challenge the Arena itself.

"Let's play then," I murmured, raising my eyes to the Witches. I was sure they were watching me.

I cautiously studied the room. Hundreds of cadavers lay on steel cots. They gave no sign of life, but I was sure they would soon wake up. There were no doors, only a big picture window offering no way out. I walked over to it and rested one hand on the glass to take a closer look. On the other side were my friends, the ones I had left on Earth.

And Assin was in the room with them.

"What the fuck?" Did they not see him? Why didn't they attack him? "Evan!" I pounded my fists on the glass, trying to warn them, but the glass shattered into a million pieces with a deafening crash.

Then, silence. On the other side of the window, an empty room. A whisper touched my ear, filling my mind: "Arise."

A grunt put me on alert and I slowly turned around. All the undead had gotten up and were staring at me with empty eye sockets. I shuddered. They weren't strangers—they were all the people I had killed during my stint as a Soldier of Death. The souls I had killed without hesitation. My brothers had always criticized me because I took our mission as a joke. To me it had been a gift. To them it had always been a curse.

In the front row were my friends.

Seeing them shook me to the core. Did that mean I had killed them too? Was that what they were trying to tell me? I backed up, shocked, and fell through the window into the next room. They followed me and surrounded me, standing there motionless with their deathly expressions and empty eyes to remind me of what I had done. They had counted on me and I had allowed myself to be killed, abandoning them to their fate.

Something flickered on the ceiling. Though it was only for a second, it was enough to remind me where I was. The Witches were playing with my mind, my sense of guilt. One of my fears was seeing my friends, my family, die. I clenched my fists, trying to drive them away. Those weren't really my friends, and I had to get out of there before all the other Champions did.

There were doors at the other end of the enormous room. All I had to do was cross through all those bodies standing between me and the exit, lined up like undead soldiers.

I got up and made my way through the corpses with familiar faces. Once again I had to leave them behind. I had to turn off my emotions. It wasn't really them.

It wasn't really them.

It wasn't really them.

My father's corpse blocked my way. I had left him too by going off to war as a volunteer. I tried to pass but he grabbed my arm and for a moment his eyes looked normal.

"Dad," I murmured.

He opened his mouth and something crawled out of his throat: a swarm of black butterflies that hit me right in the face. I kicked my father away but all the bodies around me opened their mouths. Within seconds the room had transformed into a black vortex that was trying to suck me up inside it. I began to run, desperately seeking a way out, but I was trapped.

I had expected to battle the other Champions, but this was a battle against myself. The most difficult one. I struck out at the living dead, knocking some of them down, but the butterflies were impossible to stop. They swarmed through the room and wounded me, covering my entire body with cuts. I had to escape, and fast.

"No," I whispered, stopping in my tracks. "No more running away." For once, I had to decide to stay. No door would lead me away from my fears. I had to face them.

I looked at the swarm of butterflies. *They* were the souls of the people I had killed. A dark portal I had to cross through. Slowly, I spread my arms. Seeming to understand, the swarm danced around me. In seconds they covered me and I fell to my knees.

It was the right command. The butterflies were my punishment. I had to welcome them in order to find redemption. My way out wasn't surrender, but acceptance.

Overpowered by their poison, I collapsed to the floor. The only way for me to live was to die. I would never get out of there by pushing them away. I had done that to the people they had once been: I'd rejected them, cast them aside, ignored them, forgotten them. I had killed them.

Now it was time for them to kill me.

THE MISSION

A strange dizziness washed over me. I opened my eyes and found myself hanging by my feet. Something odd was going on, though: the rest of the world wasn't upside-down. Beside me was a desk, a chair, cabinets. It all seemed normal apart from the fact that I was dangling toward the ceiling and not toward the ground. It was as though everything was responding to an inverted force of gravity that left only me unaffected.

I bent at the waist and tried to free myself from the chains, but couldn't.

Then I saw it, the small key lying below my head on the ceiling.

"You've got to be kidding," I groaned. I reached out, but it was no use. It was too far away. There was no time for these little games. I bent double again and tried to break the chains, but they were so tight they were leaving marks.

I swung toward the desk next to me. A long nail rested on it. I picked it up. Maybe with that I could reach the key. I tried, but after a few attempts all I managed to do was push it farther away. I bent over again and tried using the nail to pry open the lock on the chains, but it was no use.

Maybe there was something hidden in the desk that would come in handy. In the Arena we didn't have powers, but with a little luck we could create them. I rifled through the drawers until I found what I needed: a remote control. I took out the battery. Fortunately it was a high-voltage one. I reached out toward a heavy metal lamp mounted on the wall and ripped it off. Yanking out the wires, sparks hitting my face in the process, I pulled out a long copper wire. Now all I needed was some tape.

I rifled through the drawers again, but evidently it wasn't my lucky day.

Or maybe it was.

A picture hung on the wall. The glass was broken. I checked the back of it and my spirits brightened: it was held together by a small strip of tape. The photograph was of Insane Souls staring at the lens, their faces covered with blood. A ghoulish choice, but I didn't care.

"Let's get moving. I've gotten through real-time strategy video games better than this." They didn't know who they were dealing with-aside from women, motorcycles, and my missions as a Subterranean, my time on Earth had primarily been devoted to playing video games. At that very moment, a huge beast rammed the glass door with all its weight. "Shit, me and my big mouth." I taped the copper wire to the nail, leaving one end free. It wasn't easy to move upside-down with a wild beast snarling on the other side of the door, desperate to gobble me up.

Fuck! There were two of them!

I wound the wire around the nail in a spiral to preserve the electromagnetic effect. The more loops the coil had, the greater the power. The wire wasn't long but it would have to do.

The glass cracked beneath the beasts' blows. I had to hurry. I scraped the two ends of the wire against my armor to expose the copper, then touched them to the two poles of the battery. I held the nail out toward the key. Drawn by the magnetic field, it moved closer and clattered against the metal. I smiled and grabbed it with my mouth, dropping my makeshift magnet.

I hurried to undo the lock trapping me as one of the beasts shattered the glass. Free, I grabbed the chains and swung myself toward the beast, kicking it with both feet. It whimpered as it crumpled to the floor. It turned out there weren't two of them after all—it was a single beast with two heads. I had knocked one of them out but the other stood its ground, its sharp fangs looking like those of a wolf that had been bitten by a vampire.

I slowly stepped back as the creature advanced. When it launched itself toward my chest I threw myself backwards, using the beast's own impetus to fling it behind me. I crawled toward the magnetic nail, but the beast attacked me again, shoving me back onto the floor. We struggled and its fangs sank into my shoulder, tearing away a piece of flesh. The pain was blinding. Screaming, I held it away from my neck while reaching for the nail attached to the battery. A powerful electric charge surged through me, forcing me to drop it. I sensed the murmur of a spirit passing me. The Witches were toying with me. One of them had definitely increased the voltage.

Now that its fangs had had a taste of my flesh, the beast grew thirsty for my blood. It was one of those moments when a little help from Kreeshna would have come in handy. Ignoring the pain from the shocks, I grabbed the nail again and drove it between the beast's eyes, the electric current surging through me. It was as though a lightning bolt had split its forehead in two. The beast tensed and fell, its body still buzzing with electricity. Wielding that nail had been like handling a thunderbolt. It seemed the Witch had read my mind: she'd increased my strength, otherwise I would have been zapped too. I scrambled back across the floor-ceiling and got to my feet. It was strange how everything was upside-down. The desk and chairs were above me, hanging from the ceiling.

Looking around, I saw something on the wall. A large safe. Grabbing hold of whatever I could, I climbed up the wall until I reached it. Distant growls drew closer in the hallway. More creatures were hunting me. I didn't have time to guess the combination.

I leaned over, wrenched the remains of the metal sconce off the wall, and struck the digital display in an attempt to crack it open. The growls were closer now and the beasts' claws rasped against the floor, eager to sink into me. If I left the room right now I might still be in time to escape them.

If the Stage Director had put a wall safe here, there must be something inside it, something important, judging from the size of the strongbox. I had to force it open some-how. I ripped the cover off the control panel and fiddled with the wires, but when I yanked one out, a metal bar slid out, sealing off the safe even more securely. A curse escaped me. I had to get out of there. It sounded like there were lots of beasts, and I couldn't take them all on at once.

Decades after I'd been killed in the war and become a Subterranean, the first video game was invented. It had been a red-letter day for me. I'd taken to gaming like a natural, and video games had become my favorite pastime —after women, of course. So it wasn't the first time I'd entered a virtual-reality environment. It was just that in this one I couldn't take off my 3-D goggles. Fighting was my only way out.

On the edge of the safe I'd noticed some writing that at first I'd mistaken for the manufacturer's details. But we were in Hell, so everything had only one manufacturer, and that was the Sisterhood. Clinging to the safe, I turned my head to read it better, ending up upside-down. "Now I know what it must feel like to be Spider-Man," I murmured, the blood rushing to my head. The engraving read:

At each knell, flakes of ash fall onto a carpet of red

"WHAT THE FUCK DOES THAT MEAN?" I certainly wasn't a poetry guy. What did flakes of ash have to do with it? Suddenly I understood. *They fall.* Like us. It was referring to the Champions. We were the ash; the carpet of red was the river of blood that would be shed. The knells were the levels. The line was talking about how many of us would fall during the trials. Or at least I hoped that was it.

I punched in the first number on the digital number pad: nine, the number of players. A metal bar slid back, telling me I was on the right track. What could the combination be? *At each knell.* How many of us would fall? I followed my instinct and pressed the number three—the number of competitors destined to lose in the first level. Another bar in the safe slid back. I continued. At that point there would be six of us left to battle it out in the second round. The third, though, was a face-off between only two players. That meant four more would be missing when the roll was called for the third and final round. I punched in the number four and the sound of another metal bar urged me on. Of the two remaining in the final level, one would fall, leaving the glory to the victor. I punched in the number one and held my breath. A click told me I'd done it.

When I swung the heavy door open, I was happy I hadn't left. A low growl broke the silence. Another of the two-headed beasts had crept into the room and was right below me. "Hi," I said to both its heads, then whipped out the gun I'd just found. "Bye," I said as I fired it, wrapping up our little chat. I stared at the gun, amazed. I'd shot a hole through both its heads.

I went back to focusing on my spoils. "I knew it was a better idea to stay." The safe was full of weapons. The other beasts were approaching, so I ransacked it, taking everything I could carry: a nail gun, a knife with a spiked handle, a compact machine gun that would definitely come in handy, and a few grenades. I examined a beautiful scythe with a skeleton carved on its handle and slung it over my shoulder. "Perfect for a Reaper Angel."

Finally, my favorite: a leather glove that looked seriously lethal. I put it on and studied my hand. There was a button in the center of the palm. I made a fist and a small crescent-shaped blade darted out and instantly retracted. Fast and deadly. Just how I liked it. My enemies wouldn't even see it coming.

All at once three beasts rushed in, skidding across the floor. Or maybe I should say six beasts, given that they each had two heads. I leapt down and ran toward them, brandishing the machine gun. When they launched themselves at me I threw myself to my knees and slid across the floor, reducing them to Swiss cheese. Only one escaped my wrath. It leapt onto the wall and began to run upside-down across the ceiling, coming dangerously close. Damn, the machine gun was out of bullets. I pulled out the nail gun, but my first shots missed the target, which moved swiftly, preparing to attack. When it leapt at me, I swung the scythe off my shoulder and slashed it through the air, chopping the beast in two.

The thud it made hitting the ground was drowned out by an ominous howl coming from the corridor. I raced out the door only to freeze in my tracks. "Fuck!" There were too many of them. Some were walking on the walls, others on the ceiling, defying the laws of physics.

Not much ammunition was left. I threw a grenade at them and sprinted in the opposite direction, turning the corner seconds before it exploded and barely dodging the blast of fire and debris.

I peeked back around the corner. The corridor was a tunnel of flames. Suddenly one of the monsters leapt out of the inferno straight at me. I reacted instinctively, firing a shot that knocked it off its course. But there were others, many others. The flames hadn't stopped them. I started running again, trying to shake them.

With each corner I turned, I was more and more convinced I was running in circles in that damned labyrinth. My suspicions were confirmed when I passed the room with the safe again: it was a prison. My mission was to figure out how to escape it. But first I had to shake the two-headed hounds of Hades.

I entered the room. I heard them coming closer, panting, howling for blood, their claws scraping the floor, grating on my nerves. The door to the safe shifted, suggesting my next move. I climbed up to the ceiling and crawled inside it, discovering it was a perfect fit.

The multitude of beasts streamed into the room and I held my breath. Luckily they were stupid. When they saw the empty room they didn't stop to look around, but instead, bounded off into the hallway, scrambling over each other to get back on my trail.

All except one.

The beast that stayed behind came closer and stopped in the center of the room, where it took its time sniffing the air. It knew I was there. Jumping onto the wall, it crept onto the ceiling just like that.

Its low growl came closer and closer. I took out the gun

and gripped it tightly when the creature's eye peered into the opening. It had found me. I prepared to shoot, but instead of nudging the safe open the beast rammed it shut with its head. The lock clicked, trapping me inside. The safe was a perfect coffin in which I had buried myself alive.

I pounded my fists against the door, trying to open it and pushed against it with my feet with all my might, gritting my teeth from the pain in my shoulder. It was no use. The bite from the hound of Hades throbbed and burned like fire. Turning into one of them was the last thing I needed.

But this wasn't a horror flick. It was a game, and I had to find my way out. I tried to pry the lock open with the blade of my knife, but I was SOL. A drop of sweat slid down my forehead. All it would take was the other Champions finding their way out before me and I would be screwed. Goodbye, Stella. If I had to lose I would rather be torn to shreds than end up trapped like a moron.

It was pitch black in the safe. I ran my hands over the walls and my fingers touched something that felt like a series of buttons. One, two, three. Identical in shape and size. I didn't know what color they were but I hoped I wouldn't press the red one. In the movies the people who pushed the red button were always fucked.

"Okay," I murmured to myself. "Choose one, Drake."

I pressed the one in the middle and a sudden commotion shook the safe. My head began to spin and I braced myself. It felt like the safe was tumbling down a hill inside a Zorb ball. When everything stopped I found myself upside down, trapped beneath my own weight. "This is why I've always hated carnival rides," I muttered.

I tried again, this time with the button on the left. A massive force plastered me to the roof of the safe as it plunged down like an elevator whose cables have snapped. I felt like a gnat hitting a windshield. When the descent ended, one of the walls opened, spilling me out onto the ground.

Man, I hoped Stella wasn't watching this. It was definitely not sexy.

I stood up cautiously and found myself in a garage full of strange, futuristic-looking cars. No one was there. Not yet, at least. I was about to walk out when I remembered there were three buttons in the safe. One was left.

Maybe I should just leave . . . or maybe not. To hell with it! I went back and pressed the last button, the one on the right. The safe lit up. I was right: it had become an elevator. The mirror on the back wall reflected my image. *Not bad.* The wound on my shoulder, though, was disgusting. Why hadn't it already healed like all the others? Were the effects of Kreeshna's blood wearing off? I studied it. Maybe the wound was too deep even for the Witch's powers.

Something glinted in the mirror, grabbing my attention. A black droplet swelled on its surface and began to slide down, followed by another. It was like the mirror was oozing demon blood.

A message appeared:

Three keys to stay in, but not to get out.
As you find them, a sacrifice must come about.
The black one is deadly, the green one is quick.

But be brave and beware of the red one's trick.

I WAS PERPLEXED as I tried to memorize the message. *It was a clue.* Three keys to stay in, but not to get out. It was talking about the first level. I had no idea what the rest meant, but one thing was clear: I had to find three keys in order to complete the mission and advance past this level. The black blood oozed down over the writing, creating a ghastly design.

The sudden wail of a car alarm made me spin around. Headlights flashed on and tires squealed ominously as a car shot toward me like a missile. I leapt to one side and it swerved to avoid crashing into the wall. By the time I got to my feet and started running, the car was chasing me again.

The garage was huge, packed with empty cars. Beautiful, unusual-looking ones. Some were streamlined, others rounded. They looked like prototypes or cars from the future. I had never seen anything like them.

To shake my pursuer, I jumped onto the car hoods and tops, but the bastard wasn't letting up. I had no idea who it was and couldn't see through the windshield. Opening the car doors didn't work—they were all locked. I smashed in a window with my elbow and climbed inside one before he arrived. It was easy enough to get it started, but a glance at the gas gauge instantly dashed my hopes.

Then I looked up and saw it: a futuristic two-wheeler straight out of my most forbidden dreams. Ever since I'd ended up in that hellhole I'd longed to get back on a motorcycle.

I crawled back through the window and leapt from roof to roof to reach it more quickly. It started up instantly. At the same moment, all the other cars in the garage started up as well, as though they'd awakened from a dream. They tried to block my way, but I reared up and raced out of the garage.

My pursuer drew even with me but I shot off, chasing the wind. The roar of my bike's engine drowned out the revving of the cars that echoed through the garage. As adrenaline pumped through my body, I looked over my shoulder. More cars had begun to chase me and that bastard was still right on my tail. I sped up even more. God, had I missed that sensation. All those late-night races against my brothers had taught me well. That Soul didn't have a chance in hell of catching up with me.

Even the scenario seemed like a futuristic movie. We passed beneath a bridge and I revved the accelerator, making the two-wheeled beast beneath me roar. When the car pulled up alongside me, the Soul at the wheel offered me a grisly smile. He wasn't Insane yet, but he was definitely well on his way.

As I watched him, his eyes flickered green, just for a second, just long enough for me to understand. The Soul accelerated and passed me. He wasn't chasing me. I was the one who had to catch *him*. That nasty son of a bitch. *He* was the key.

LEVELING UP

The first level was a chase, then. No one but a Witch could have thought of hiding the keys *inside* the Damned. The only way to get the first one—the green one —was to kill him, but the bastard was fast. Just like the clue said.

I accelerated and the motorcycle reared up. It wasn't difficult to pull up next to him, since I was good at hot pursuits, but just when I reached peak speed the car took off, disappearing from sight.

Who the fuck was he? Toretto? I would never catch him. Furious, I looked down at the bike and noticed a button. It was red, as I had feared. Challenging fate, I pressed it. The front wheel lifted off the ground and the bike zoomed off like a missile.

When I got close to the Green Lantern, a group of motorcycles raced in my direction, trying to catch me. I tilted my bike and skidded into them. Pressing the button again, I continued the chase, the front tire rising up with a roar.

The road in front of us suddenly veered upward, curling into a spectacular loop-the-loop that we could only complete without losing traction by going at top speed. My adversary sped up, making his intentions clear. I followed him without hesitation. The hardest part was letting go of the bike. When I reached the very top of the loop, I released my grip on the handlebars and leapt into the void. As planned, I crashed down onto the hood of his car. Man, did that hurt! I gasped for breath. That wasn't how I'd imagined the landing.

I watched the motorcycle crash to the ground, then turned toward the Soul behind the windshield. "You'll pay for this."

He swerved, trying to throw me off the car. Time to pull out the nail gun. Only one shot was left, but I didn't care. I squeezed the trigger and the nail lodged in the windshield, forming a thick spider web of cracks. Instead of braking, as I'd expected, the car accelerated even more. My body slammed against the windshield, sending shards flying.

I found myself inside the car. The Soul looked at me, his gaze devoid of humanity. *Fuck, was he ugly.* "Wanna give me a lift?" I grabbed him by the back of the head and smashed his corpse-like face into the dashboard over and over.

The car spun around and headed down a street. I could see it came to an abrupt end scant yards ahead of us. *Shit.* I grabbed the Soul and dragged him out of the moving car a millisecond before it flew into the void. We tumbled to the ground, rolling to a stop, but I shot to my feet instantly to avoid losing my advantage. I punched him in the face and held him tight, afraid he would escape.

Beyond the edge of the cliff, the car burst into a chain reaction of explosions. The blast was deafening and the heat burned my skin. The Soul opened his mouth to scream but didn't have the chance. His face burned to cinders and disintegrated, his eyes glimmering green before the wind whirled his ashes away.

Disoriented, I frowned. His threadbare jacket was still in my fist, but not a trace of him was left. I rifled through his pockets and felt something. Was it the key? I quickly pulled it out. It was burning hot and didn't look like a key, just a piece of curved metal. Its green glow, however, made it perfectly clear: *I'd found it.*

The glow faded, confirming that I was right.

There were two left.

I looked up. The scenario had changed. No more futuristic landscape. Now it looked more like an episode of *The Walking Dead.* There was an overpass with cars on it, but they were all just sitting there abandoned, their doors open, as though everyone had unexpectedly run off. There was even the wreckage of a helicopter that had crashed into an overturned bus. I dragged myself to my feet and set off walking toward a city I glimpsed on the horizon.

No fuel in the gas tanks, but I found something even more precious: munitions. I reloaded all my weapons and leaned against a car to catch my breath, wondering how my opponents were making out. I looked up at the sky, where I knew the Witches were watching us. Their spirits weren't really up there, though. They were with us, around us. Everywhere. I could hear them whispering in my head as they studied my moves, exploited my weaknesses, decided on gaming strategies. Or maybe they were there only to confuse me. The spectators were watching us on the screens, but the Witches were inside the Arena, just outside the game, invisible to our eyes but an integral part of the challenges. Close enough to hinder us. It was like playing against the computer, except that the difficulties—even the configuration of the Arena itself—weren't predetermined. Instead they were being crafted specifically for me. Only one of them was playing in my favor. In all likelihood I wouldn't have gotten as far as I had without Kreeshna's blood in my veins. It had given me strength, healed my wounds, kept me from dying like in some stupid video game. And yet it took decision-making to win a war—and that was entirely up to me.

I didn't know if Kreeshna was giving the other Champions a run for their money like the other Sisters were doing with me. Still, she definitely hadn't been helping me out all that much. I raised my breastplate and saw a long gash across my side. I must have cut myself on the broken windshield when I dove into the car. Throwing back my head, I took several deep breaths.

The Witch must have sensed my agony because a wave of warmth pervaded me. I felt her blood boil in my veins. She was inside my head like a whispered sigh that I couldn't make out. Before my eyes, the wound began to close up and the pain subsided. The one on my shoulder, though, gave no sign of healing.

Fuck you, I thought. I was used to counting only on myself. I didn't need her.

I resigned myself and set off walking toward the city. The buildings were in ruins, the streets deserted and reduced to a cluster of slums. A shadow darted past me as swiftly as a ghost. I stayed on my guard until it passed me again, then followed it, clambering over the rubble in the street, until it vanished. It was the Soul I was looking for, I was sure of it. The next key. I just had to find it.

All at once the blare of the horn shattered the eerie silence. For a moment I stood motionless as its echo drifted away. One of the Champions had already collected all three keys and made it through the first level. How was that possible?

I sensed a presence at my back and spun around to find it right behind me. The Soul's eyes glittered black. It was the key! I whipped out my dagger to stab it, but a spurt of black blood shot from its mouth.

"What the fuck?"

A long blade protruded from its chest a second before the Soul burst into a cloud of ash. Now I could see his killer behind him. It was another Champion. That meant we weren't in different scenarios any more, but in a single shared virtual reality.

It wasn't just any Champion either. I clenched my fists and Assin smiled at me, catching the black key on the tip of his sword. "Sorry, I saw him first." I moved to attack him but the horn blew again. We both looked up as the sound diminished along with our hopes of winning the tournament.

"You'd better hurry," Assin suggested with a smirk. He was ahead—I'd only found one key and he was already on his second. Leaping back, he landed at the foot of a mountain of debris.

I gave chase, but a distant commotion made the ground shake beneath my feet. At the end of the road a horde of ferocious gorillas appeared, charging straight at me. Their eyes gleamed ice-blue in the twilight. Squinting at them, I saw one had black eyes. He was my key. And he was ready to crush me.

All at once something clamped around my ankle, sealing it in an iron grip.

"What the hell?!"

I looked down at a hand that had burst out from the debris to hold me still. The gorillas were almost there and I was about to be trampled. There were too many of them! I tried to break free but the grip was too strong. It must be another of the Witches' attempts to hinder me. Now that there were fewer tickets to victory, they'd probably decided to play dirty. Was this their plan to get rid of me? I braced for impact, but suddenly the hand pulled me down through the debris into an underground cave.

I shot to my feet, instantly alert. Whoever it was that had dragged me down there was really strong. I might even have thanked them for saving me from the gorillas' fury if it wasn't for the fact that they had to have brought me there to kill me.

I looked around. It was a hiding place, with rags positioned here and there over openings looking out onto a street. Inside it was difficult to see. The shadow of a huge creature as massive as a tank loomed over me. The monster lit a torch, and a sigh of relief escaped me.

"Gurdan! What on earth are you doing here?"

"Gurdan save princess. Gorilla crush you." He smashed his fist into his palm to illustrate.

I was amazed. "Did you create this hideaway down here?"

"Hide good better than hunt good."

"I've got to get out of here. One of the gorillas has flickering black eyes. It has the key and I need to kill it!"

"You wait," the ogre told me, motioning me closer. He pulled aside a small cloth, showing me what was going on outside. Huge apes were everywhere. The Damned had poured into the streets and various Champions were pulverizing them to gain an advantage. One of them was battling three Souls when a gorilla picked him up and hurled him far away. Another Champion vanished before my eyes: he must have just found his third key. The horn sounded again, even louder inside the cramped space.

The ogre towered over me, bigger than ever. Was he another of the Witches' tricks to slow me down? I didn't have time for this.

"I can't stay here. I need to act fast!"

"Gurdan help," he insisted. It was comical: an ogre offering me his help against a horde of gorillas.

"I don't want your help. You'll get yourself killed!" Why had the Witches thrown him into the Arena? I knew how much Stella cared about him, but I couldn't afford to think about his safety right now.

Maybe that was the Witches' plan: to distract me from my objective.

Just then, Gurdan punched through the debris and pulled in someone else. Or rather, *something* else. My eyes widened when I saw the gorilla's nostrils flare. It was clearly disoriented. Without giving it the chance to get up, the ogre pounded on its chest with both fists, smashing it to pieces. I was stunned to see the huge animal disintegrate.

"Gurdan help," he repeated after a moment of silence.

"You've convinced me," I said, still shocked by the ogre's brutality. I'd better not talk back to him.

I searched the floor for the key, but it wasn't there. This one hadn't been the gorilla I was looking for. My target was still out there somewhere. The horn sounded again. How many of them had already finished the level? Time was running out.

"This way." The ogre lit up a passageway with his torch and motioned for me to follow him. We wound through a tunnel that was clearly below street level because I could hear the giant apes' heavy footfalls overhead. From time to time I also heard low hisses. I felt strangely confused, in danger of losing my focus. It was them, the Witches, searching my mind.

"We've got to go back outside. How do you plan to help me if we stay down here? The key is up there!"

"Shh," he said. He seemed to be listening for something. On the ground above us we could hear the sound of a single gorilla. Gurdan punched through the ceiling and a patch of earth crumbled over our heads.

I laughed. "An ogre's hand popping out of the ground? That's so *Night of the Living Dead*." We were in Hell, after all.

"Talk too much, you," he reproved me.

"It's a family curse."

The roof above us caved in when Gurdan dragged the beast down. Its ice-blue eyes glinted when it growled at me, threatening to tear me to shreds with its sharp teeth. This one wasn't the key either, damn it all. Gurdan annihilated it all the same with one of his lethal blows.

Another giant ape peered through the hole above us and grabbed my companion by his bald head. "Gurdan!" I shouted. The beast yanked him up and flung him far away. I climbed out and the blood turned to ice in my veins. I was surrounded.

The gorilla that had picked Gurdan up snorted. Its dark eyes were watchful. It wasn't a beast at the mercy of its instincts, it was intelligent and was studying me.

I unslung the long scythe from my shoulder and was ready when the first one charged. I dodged its attack with a backflip and ran it through with my deadly blade. Next, three apes attacked at once. I charged at them, taking them by surprise, and chopped off their heads with one blow. A chorus of enraged shrieks united to form a single howl. The rest of the gorillas seemed to have realized it wasn't wise to wait their turn, so they all attacked at once.

"Shit," I muttered, clenching my jaw. There were too many of them.

Gurdan reappeared. He dove into the fray, picking some of them up. I pulled out the gun and aimed at their fore-heads. I didn't miss a shot. The gorillas fell like pawns on a chessboard. When I ran out of bullets, I tossed the gun aside and rushed into the crowd, slashing throats and stabbing temples with my dagger.

Finally I met its black eyes: the gorilla with the key. I leapt down from the back of one of its followers who fell to the ground after tasting my blade.

The mighty ape faced me, waiting. The strongest, most intelligent, most prized one of them all. The last one standing, whom all the others had protected at the cost of their lives.

It stood there, its eyes fixed on me as I charged it with a war cry, my dagger unsheathed. Suddenly its eyes flickered blue. I stopped in my tracks, disoriented. Something dragged the ape out of my path, hurling him away. It was Gurdan, and his eyes were suddenly as black as oil.

"No . . ." I murmured in shock.

He was the key. And to get it I would have to kill him.

THE HARDEST CHOICE

Gurdan ran to me, proud he'd gotten rid of the last gorilla. I backed away, tightening my grip on the dagger. He seemed confused by my reaction. Did he mean to kill me as well? I couldn't be sure. The Witches were rigging the game. They were our common enemy, but right now they were toying with us, making us slaughter each other.

"Gurdan save princess." He laughed and stepped toward me. Despite his massive size and deep ogre voice, he seemed like an overgrown child.

"Gurdan." I held out my hand to stop him. "Your eyes."

He touched his eyes as though that might help him understand. Gurdan had no idea what the Witches had in store for him, no idea why they'd tossed him into the Arena. Not to help me, like he thought, but to prove to everyone how selfish I'd always been. I should never have let him come with me in search of the Castle. When they'd captured me, Gurdan had disappeared. I'd fooled myself into thinking the Witches didn't care about him, but I was wrong. They had decided to use him against me.

So this was the sacrifice I would have to make to pass the trial.

I hid the knife behind my back. I didn't want him to see it and realize what I was about to do. How I wished Stella was there beside me. The Witches knew I would keep playing their dirty game if it meant saving her. I was willing to do anything for her. They also knew that deep down I'd always been selfish. Even so, Gurdan didn't deserve to die because of me.

The black one is deadly. The words from the clue echoed in my mind. Gurdan was deadly and had proved it. There was no doubt he was the key, and suddenly he seemed to realize it.

I could have shot him with the nail gun and claimed my victory, but I wasn't going to give the Witches the satisfaction of seeing me kill one of my last remaining friends in cold blood. I would face him fair and square, and the stronger of us would win.

"I'm sorry," I said softly.

The ogre came toward me, his footsteps heavy. I prepared to block his lethal blow but instead he pushed me out of the way a split second before a spear hit him in the throat, sending him flying backwards.

"No!" I shouted. I fired two rounds at the Soul who had

killed him, then rushed to the ogre and knelt at his side. "Gurdan, no! What did you do?"

"Keep promise. Gurdan help princess," he said in a broken voice.

"You stupid ogre, you didn't have to die for me." I pressed my hands against his wound, from which black blood was spurting. There was no way to save him—the spear had also lacerated the skin under his ear—but he had saved *me*. Again.

"Now," he gurgled. He was trying to say something. "Now you keep promise. Save Kahlena." I nodded and a tear slid down my cheek as he disintegrated into ash.

The key clattered to the ground but I didn't pick it up right away. After a moment its black glow faded. It too was nothing more than a piece of shapeless metal. Clutching it in my hand, I looked up to where the Witches were watching the game. They would pay for this too.

In the end, I hadn't been the one to make the sacrifice the trial demanded. Gurdan had sacrificed himself for me. In giving me the second key he had given me his life, and there I'd been, prepared to kill him. The Witches were right. I was a selfish asshole. Would Stella ever forgive me? I felt like a worm. If there was something I could still do, it was make sure he hadn't died in vain.

The key was burning in my hand, reminding me that time was of the essence. I got up, trying to count how many times the horn had sounded. How many Champions had already found all three keys? If I remembered correctly, four of them had already leveled up. Only two spots left. There would be time to grieve Gurdan's loss. Right now I had to find the last key.

The sound of shots made me turn around.

It was my gun, the one I'd dropped on the field, thinking it was out of bullets. Dumb move, in an Arena full of Souls out to kill me. Three of them approached, looking threatening. The one brandishing my gun aimed it right at my face.

"Okay, okay!" I found myself with my back against a wall and raised my hands. "We can make a deal, no need to get angry. What do you want?"

"It's your weapons we're wanting."

"What?"

"Your weapons. Swerds, guns, knives. Ammunition too." One of them, who was toothless and had only one tuft of hair left on his head, leaned over and whispered something into the ear of the first one, who continued with his demands. "And the scythe on your back. Everything. Give it to us!"

"All right," I said accommodatingly. "I'll give them to you."

The three nodded nervously. I felt kind of sorry for them. They looked like three hapless guys desperately trying to survive. Slowly lowering my hands, I pretended to go along with them but instead swiped the gun out of the first one's hand and broke his nose with my elbow.

"Sorry, asshole. This is mine." I put the gun away and drove two daggers into his temples. The second one attacked me and got a blade under the chin. His eyes went wide and he fell to the ground. The last one, the one who'd wanted my scythe, stood there, frozen. I took the weapon off my back and ran my thumb down the blade. "So you like my scythe, do you?" His eyes moved from me to the blade and then back to me, terrified. "Boo!" I exclaimed. He let out a shriek and ran off as fast as his legs could carry him.

I smiled, but my moment of triumph didn't last long. Like ants, hundreds of Souls poured onto the battlefield. No, they weren't Souls. They were shadows, and some of the other Champions were battling them. It could only mean one thing: somewhere among them was the key to the way out.

I set off running, ready to jump into the fray, when a shadow passed me, flickering red for a second.

The last key.

I changed course and chased the shadow. It took off down an alley, but when I turned the corner it was deserted. Something overhead caught my attention. I scanned the buildings and spotted the shadow leaning out of a window a few floors above, its red eyes peering down at me.

The horn sounded again and I cut my hand on a broken window. "Fuck," I cursed between gritted teeth, not because of the wound—with Witch's blood in me it would quickly heal—but because the shadow had disappeared. I entered the building. The floor lurched upward. It looked like a bomb had exploded inside.

Suddenly, through a window, I saw the shadow darting through the building across from me. It was insane. I'd seen it several floors up. How had it gotten into the other build-ing? I picked up a wooden beam that had fallen from the ceiling and connected the two buildings through a hole in the wall. The wood was splitting and I wasn't sure it would hold my weight, but I hoped it would at least last long enough for me to cross.

I had to act fast. I took a running start and leapt onto the beam, but the shadow pushed it away on the other end and I tumbled into the void. I grabbed hold of an electrical cable just in time. Fortunately the power was down in the area. I dangled there and then swung myself up through a window.

Once again my target had disappeared, but it couldn't be far away. I advanced further into the building. I glimpsed it as it disappeared around a wall to the right, but when I rounded the corner all I found was empty space. It was as though the building had been chopped in half. Peering down, I saw a swarm of shadows climbing the buildings, crawling toward me.

Instead of turning back, I clung to the side of the building and lowered myself. When I was close to the ground I jumped the rest of the way and hid in a side street. I couldn't take on so many of them all at once. More importantly, I didn't want to. Not if my key wasn't among them.

I didn't have much time. I clutched my dog tag. A Mizhya had tried to take it off me before the beginning of the tournament, but I had pointed my knife at her throat.

The last horn had to sound for me. Otherwise I would lose my Stella forever.

I leaned back against the wall. The grunts of the other shadows were close. Were they Damned Souls? Infernal beasts? Ethereal shadows my blade wouldn't be able to bring down? That wouldn't be surprising, coming from the Witches. The last key would be the hardest, but I was ready.

I sensed a flicker of movement overhead and looked up. My target was above me. Crouched on a low wall, it leapt down, but I was faster. Grabbing it by the ankle, I yanked it back, gripped it by the shoulders and slammed it against the wall. When our eyes met, my world crumbled at my feet.

It wasn't a shadow. It was Stella.

A PROMISE WITH A BITTER TASTE

"Stella!" I embraced her, holding her tight, and my lips instantly found hers. I felt like a desperate wanderer who had finally found his way home. I cupped her face in my hands but her gaze grew ice-cold and a second later her blade was at my throat. "Stella, what are you doing?"

"My name is Kahlena. I've told you a thousand times."

"Why are you here? Why did they throw you into the Arena?" My goal was to make sure Stella's life was safe, but how could I do that if she was there too? What game were the Witches playing?

"I *chose* to enter the game," she said, leaving me baffled.

"Why would you do that? How can I save you if I need to protect you?"

"I've never needed your protection."

I disarmed her and pinned her wrists to the wall, forcing her to look me in the eye. "Stella, this isn't a competition between the two of us. I'm competing *for* you. To earn your freedom."

"You're wrong. I'm competing now too. One on one. I've decided to earn my freedom on my own."

I stepped back, bewildered. "What are you talking about? Did they brainwash you? Now I get why they forced you to become a Mizhya—so they could pit you against me."

"They didn't force me to do anything." As quick as lightning she snatched the knives from my belt, pointing one at the front of my neck and the other at my nape. I'd seen her make that move before. It was deadly. "You, on the other hand, took advantage of me."

"What?!"

"First you left me to slowly go insane in Hell. Then, just when I'd found a happy medium between reason and madness, you came back to torture me. It's your fault that they tore me away from my hiding place, that they kidnapped and killed my allies." Stella shoved me back and struck a defensive pose. "They forced me to subjugate myself. *You're* the cause of all this."

"You're angry," I said, dodging her first attack, "but this will all be over soon, and you and I will be able to leave the Castle. No one will come looking for us. We'll be free. Free to pick up where we left off. Free to love each other."

"Love each other." Stella laughed, mocking my words. "I saw your idea of *love* when you stuck your tongue into Kreeshna's mouth right before my eyes." She attacked me again but I spun her around and pinned her face to the wall.

"Stop talking bullshit. I was under her spell!"

Stella kicked my legs out from under me and I wound up on the floor. She dug her foot into my chest. "It wasn't the first time it had happened. You know, when you become one of the Witches' she-warriors, you get to know lots of things. Including how you spent your time when you were at the Castle. Commitment really isn't your strong point, is it? Khetra and I ended up making friends."

"Stella, this is no time for jealousy. Our survival's at stake!" I shouted. I tried to get up, but she shoved me down again.

"You killed Gurdan!" she screamed, shattering all my defenses.

"I didn't want it to happen. I'm sorry!"

"You know what Kreeshna told me, after your kiss? She told me I should be grateful because when all this is over she's going to let me watch you make love to her every night."

"That's never going to happen. It's insane. You're talking nonsense." I broke free and somersaulted to my feet, back on my guard.

"I'd rather kill you myself than take the risk." She was so nimble I didn't see it coming when she whisked the scythe from my shoulder, fast as a shadow.

"Stella, it's all the Witches' fault, can't you see that? They're manipulating us, even right now."

"No. They're right. I can't put my freedom in your hands. You've never even won an Opalion." My eyes widened, my pride wounded. Stella didn't believe in me. "It doesn't matter, though. They've offered me another way out," she confessed. "If I kill you, they'll let me go."

I staggered back, my mind reeling. While I was out battling for her, she was plotting to get rid of me to earn her freedom? Nothing made sense any more. The Witches were definitely scheming to get me eliminated, but I wasn't about to play along. "I'm not going to fight you," I said.

"Everything's going to end just as it began."

"With an arrow in my chest? News flash: you just shot one right into my heart."

"I'm sorry. I've made up my mind." She took a running start and with an acrobatic leap flew through the air. I dodged her blade just in time. *She was serious.* I continued to dodge her blows and counterattacked. I didn't want to hurt her, but she had become too skilled.

"Stella, stop!"

"Fight, you coward!" she screamed. I was shocked. I had never seen her so furious before.

All at once, something happened, something worse than death: her eyes flickered, red as dawn.

"No . . ." I gasped, retreating. I tripped and fell to the ground. What twisted trick were the Witches playing on us? Stella was the last key. I would have to kill her to get past this level, but what sense would that make?

For me, the game ended here. I'd only been fighting for her and would rather die than take her life. The Witch who had put her into play had studied her moves well.

Stella stood over me, brandishing the scythe. Rising to my knees, I rested my throat against the blade. I looked up at the sky, toward the Witches. To them this was all a game. Our lives didn't matter. For me, it was Game Over.

"Kill me if you have to," I said softly, every hope I'd

cherished for us vanishing like a puff of smoke. *Tournament, my ass.* By hiding the key inside Stella the Witches had deprived me of any possible chance of victory. "I'm going to keep my promise and die for you." Maybe this was the sacrifice the clue was actually referring to.

"Goodbye," she said. My mind filled with memories: her laughter echoing through the grotto, her cheek against my chest after we'd made love. A tear trickled down my cheek as her voice filled my head.

Were you with other women while I was gone?

No one who mattered.

So yes.

You've already shot me once. We'd better not dredge up the past too much.

Relax, big talker. Angry jealousy is for the weak . . . the weak . . . the weak . . .

I raised my eyes to Stella. I'd seen the disappointment on her face when I kissed Kreeshna, but the hatred I saw in her eyes right now wasn't her. She was stronger and prouder than this.

Suddenly I remembered: the third clue wasn't about sacrifice. It was about courage.

"Are you prepared to die for me, Drake?"

"Of course." I snatched the knife off the floor and shot to my feet, planting it in her heart. "But not in this level."

My game wasn't over yet.

Though I was more than willing to sacrifice myself for her, I'd finally realized what was going on. Stella would never say those things. She would never take sides against me just out of jealousy. That wasn't Stella. It was another of the Witches' tricks. It was all deception. Kreeshna wanted me to level up as much as I did, so she would never have sent in Stella. It had to be a move by her adversaries to get rid of me. That meant they were afraid enough of me to want to avoid facing me. Whoever it was, she'd taken it for granted that it was normal to kill one's own love out of jealousy. The Witches knew everything about possession but nothing about love. The freedom to love was a concept they didn't understand.

The dagger lodged in her heart, Stella grimaced and her red eyes lengthened like a serpent's. There was no doubt about it: this was the work of one of the Witches. Stella's face disintegrated like dust in the wind.

The key clattered to floor. It was a red crescent. I knelt and picked it up, then looked up again, defiantly raising it toward the Witches.

But be brave and beware of the red one's trick. If it was bravery they'd wanted me to demonstrate, I'd just overcome my trial.

I had the third key.

LEVEL ONE

I stood there waiting for the horn to sound, but it didn't happen. Why was I still there? I had all three keys, I should have moved on to the next level. Had another Champion beat me to it? Had I not noticed the horn because I was so wrapped up in Stella? Or had I counted wrong?

A sudden sound put me on alert. I leapt over the alley wall and my eyes bulged: shadows had filled all the streets. There was no way out. Now that they were closer I could see them clearly. They were every child's nightmare, the shadow lurking under the bed. I could see through their bodies and their faces were like masks frozen in an eternal scream.

The other Champions were still there in the heat of battle, cutting off the heads of the shadows, reducing them to ash. Without thinking twice, I joined the fray. Unless I was mistaken, there was still one spot left on the chariot to victory, and I couldn't afford to miss it.

Pulling out my heavy artillery, I strode toward the crowd, firing nonstop with both hands. Shadows collapsed to the ground, clearing a path. I slowly turned in a circle, my arms spread wide and my fingers squeezing both triggers. I was tired and wounded, but with Kreeshna's blood in my body I felt invincible. Or maybe it was desperation that was making me feel that way. I couldn't lose. Not now.

Once my ammo was used up I unsheathed the daggers and plowed through the shadows, taking on the damned bastards and anybody else who got in my way. Black blood drenched me as I bellowed, drowning out the sounds of the battle. It was a roar of rage I could no longer contain. Rage toward the puppeteers pulling my strings, rage over Gurdan. Rage over Stella. Even though I knew it hadn't really been her, seeing her die beneath my blade had broken me in half. If I'd let her kill me I would have lost, condemning her. I hadn't saved Stella yet, but at least I still had the chance to do it. I hated the Witches even more for forcing me to witness what would happen if I didn't win. Our lives were at stake and I knew Stella would die before my eyes.

A shadow darted past me. I raced after it, but another Champion blocked my way and struck it down first. We found ourselves face to face, but it wasn't time for us to battle each other yet. It would have been a pointless waste of time. Our most pressing challenge right now was getting past this level.

He nodded to me, then dove back into the thick of the

battle. Three keys dangled from his armor. He too had found them all but was still trapped here. Like me.

We had to get out, but how? Disoriented, I stopped to look around. I'd assumed that the keys would be used to open a lock, but there were no doors of any kind anywhere. What did the Witches want us to do? Killing all the shadows would be impossible. It was just a waste of time. For every one I took down, two more appeared.

I was surrounded. "What do you expect me to do?!" I screamed at the sky. "How the hell do I find the way out?!" A shadow scratched my back. I grabbed it by the throat and raised it off the ground. Another one sank its teeth into the wound on my shoulder and I howled in pain. I turned to annihilate it, but something about its face had changed. It wasn't translucent like the others any more. It was material- izing, its eyes lengthening. Though it had been hideous before, now—with half a shadow face—it was absolutely horrific.

I stood stock-still as it grabbed me by the shoulders. "We are our own way out," it gurgled, its voice as deep as a curse. It let go of me and exploded into a myriad of pieces. I began to understand what had happened. The shadow had drunk Kreeshna's blood from my wound. That was why it had begun to solidify, but then hadn't survived.

Staggering back, I felt a shiver run down my spine. *We are our own way out.* What did that mean? I sank to my knees, overwhelmed by the urgency of the mission I couldn't accomplish. My shoulder burned like fire. I clutched at the ground as other shadows attempted to tear the flesh from my bones. Would this be my end? The end of everything? I didn't care about dying, but I couldn't bear the thought that this time Stella wouldn't forgive me.

I'd given it my all. I had found the keys. But I hadn't managed to get out.

Get out.

Get out.

Get out.

The words echoed through my head. *Three keys to stay in but not to get out.* I gritted my teeth against the constantly throbbing ache in my shoulder. A white-hot fire was devouring me, keeping me from thinking straight. Why wasn't Kreeshna healing the wound?

Suddenly I had an idea. I took out the keys and laid them on the ground. Each had a different shape. The first one looked like a lump of curved metal, the second coiled around itself with a tapered end, making it resemble a tail. But it was when I examined the third one that I understood. It was flattened, like a head. They weren't three separate keys but rather, three parts of a whole. I moved them closer and they began to tremble, drawn to each other. They snapped together, forming an emblem: a Dakor, the Witches' serpent.

A shiver of enthusiasm ran through me as the last piece of the puzzle fell into place: the metal Dakor was the same shape as the wound in my shoulder. *We are our own way out.* The solution had been there all along. That was why the Witch's blood hadn't healed me. I brought the trinket close to my shoulder and the serpent sprang to life, confirming my theory. The wound throbbed like a summons. My eyes bulged as the creature slithered over my skin and nestled its body into the wound left by the bite. It was a perfect fit for the key.

It was ironic that the Witches had included a trial like this for us to pass to the next level. The Dakor were forever lurking in their flesh. Seeing a serpent enter a Subterranean must have been amusing for the Sisterhood. Satisfying, even. It was the millionth demonstration of their dominion over us. But if they thought I cared about that even one little bit, they were wrong. For Stella, I would have eaten the Dakor if that was what it took.

A shudder ran through me and I rose to my feet. The shadows pulled back and exploded, forming a single massive cloud of black dust around me. All at once, each particle froze in midair as though someone had hit the pause button. The landscape around me dissolved into millions of pixels that vanished on the wind, whisking away the virtual reality.

I found myself back in the Arena. The horn sounded for the last spot. Mine. A voice filled my head.

Level one complete.

THE COURAGE OF THOSE WHO REMAIN

The crowd burst into cheers when I made my appearance in the Arena. The walls that had sucked us into the virtual reality were once again surrounding the battlefield. My face on the screens showed everyone the last Champion to make it through. A list of statistics appeared beside my image as though I really were a character in a video game—only I was real. My wounds stung and my hands were covered with the blood of those who had gotten in my way.

In addition to vital stats like my energy level and the amount of lymphe remaining in my body, other scores appeared next to my name, corresponding to the abilities I had demonstrated: *Speed: 8. Resilience: 9.* These were followed by others, including *Ingenuity, Stoicism, and Heroism.* Finally, *Bravery: 10.* The highest score possible.

Some abilities had no scores next to them: *Mental endurance. Physical endurance. Strength.*

Hadn't I already proven those? What were the Witches expecting? What trial did they plan to subject us to? We weren't allowed to know in advance what kind of trial we were about to face, but I suspected the crowd could see it from our scores on the screen.

A drum roll brought my mind back to the Arena.

On the screens, some of the charts faded away: those of the Champions I'd left behind by leveling up before them. Their Witches' thrones quickly descended, eliminating them from the game. The vanquished Witches immediately transformed into panthers and began to patrol the Arena.

I memorized my opponents' scores, their strengths and weaknesses. Under the heading *Self-sacrifice,* one of them had a score of one. The bastard. I wondered who or what else he had destroyed to save his own ass.

On the charts of the disqualified players I'd noticed that some of them hadn't been successful in their bravery trial. I had faced Stella. I wondered what they had come up against. In a single Arena, nine different trials. We had all been pawns in the same game, but the real battle had been waged inside our minds. To each his own challenge. And I had gotten through them all.

I looked at Kreeshna, who was still sitting high above on her throne of power. Her eyes were waiting for mine, shining with pride. Being victorious over her Sisters mattered more to her than anything else.

For a brief moment the screens panned the crowd, which was in a frenzy over the Champions who had made it.

Suddenly they stopped on Stella's face. Our eyes locked as though she were really right next to me. A wave of emotion gripped my chest at seeing her still alive, her eyes full of hope. She was counting on me. She trusted me, trusted that I would save her. I had no intention of letting her down.

When her image disappeared I turned to look for her, desperate, but the only people in the Arena were the Champions, separated from everyone else by the giant screens. The thought that she was on the other side of them made me nervous. I balled my hands into fists to keep myself from scaling them barehanded to reach her. I might even have done it, but that would be signing our death sentence.

On the Panthior, the platform of honor above the center of the Arena, Sophìa rose from her throne and the crowd held its breath. Slowly she clapped her hands. The sound echoed through the Arena as black butterflies fluttered around her.

"The bravest, the fastest, the cleverest. The six most valiant Champions of the Tournament have my admiration. With their abilities they have demonstrated that they know how to survive in any perilous situation." The screens showed the charts of the six remaining Champions and then mixed them up, grouping us together, three against three. "They are the finest of the finest," Sophìa went on. "The time has come for them to battle one other."

The crowd went wild, eager to watch us fight each other to the death. The bastard who had sent me to Hell was still in the Tournament. Good. I couldn't wait to annihilate him.

The Empress clapped her hands a final time and the

screens withdrew into the ground. The Damned burst into cheers at finally seeing us in the flesh.

I looked around desperately for Stella. I knew she was there among the she-warriors, but there were too many of them. I couldn't find her.

A commotion caught my attention and I saw her. She pushed her way through the other Mizhyas. They blocked her path, but she broke free and beat the she-warriors back with a staff, knocking to the ground anyone who got in her way. She threw the weapon down and ran toward me.

At the same instant, I saw a panther eyeing her.

"Stella, no!" It would tear her to pieces if she got close to the Arena. Without thinking twice, I raced toward her. As soon as Stella stepped onto the battlefield, the panther launched its attack, bounding toward her, claws out.

"No!!!" I screamed, flinging myself at the animal. I knew that behind its appearance was a Witch and that I had no chance against her. A single scratch from her poisoned claws and I would be out for the count, but I didn't care. I grasped the panther around the belly and tumbled across the ground with it. Getting to my knees, I quickly withdrew my hands. I hadn't gone over the edge yet.

The crowd was paralyzed in the stands: Stella was inside the Arena. She had crossed the borderline. The panther rose up, ready to attack her again, but I shielded Stella with my body. Kreeshna stood up from her throne. For her, every-thing was at stake, but would her blood be enough to give me the strength to defeat one of her Sisters?

"Halt!" We all turned toward the Empress. "Kreeshna's Champion has proved his valor. However, the tournament is not yet over and this may well be these two lovers' final farewell. We shall grant them one last moment together."

The stands cheered, surprised to finally discover what I was fighting for. Kreeshna didn't seem pleased, but didn't protest. After all, it was better than letting her Sister devour me, eliminating me from the game.

"Nausyka, step aside." Vexed, the panther growled, but left the Arena. It had a ring of white fur around its left ear, and its blue eyes glittered defiantly.

I turned to Stella and practically smothered her in my arms. It felt like an eternity since the last time I'd held her close, the last time I had felt so complete and at peace. I wasn't willing to give up that sensation.

"Drake," she murmured, stroking the wounds on my arm.

I cupped her face in my hands and rested my forehead against hers. "This isn't goodbye, I promise."

A tear slid down her cheek as she nodded. I kissed her and she whispered "I love you" against my lips, breaking my heart.

"Shh . . ." I couldn't bear the note of farewell in her voice. "Tell me that when I come back," I said softly.

She tore a strip off the hem of her shirt and wound it around my arm, resting her forehead against it.

"I'm doing great. I'll kick everybody's ass. You'll see."

A faint smile curved her lips. "Speaking of which, you should watch it with the profanity."

"Me? Profanity? I *never* swear. Which screen have you been watching me on?!" I joked.

The horn sounded.

I held her tight, not wanting the moment to end, but a group of Mizhyas entered the field and tore her away from me.

"Drake!" she cried, tears streaking her face. She struggled as they dragged her away. I couldn't look at her. A tear slid painfully down my face, seeping into my heart. I hung my head. The thought of saying goodbye to her forever was unbearable. The horn sounded again and I clenched my fists, turning to face the center of the Arena.

"Good luck, Champions," Sophìa said. "*Gahl sum keht.*"

The warriors stepped back, bewildered, as the ground dissolved into millions of pixels, sucking us into the void. The second level had begun.

MAY EACH FORGE HIS GLORY

The entire floor of the Arena had cracked open, sending us tumbling into space. Announced by a tremor in the ground, a dome slowly rumbled closed over us, isolating us again from the spectators. The curved glass surface had the images of the Champions still competing projected onto it. We were like white mice in a labyrinth of death.

Our skills had determined who was on each team. Six contestants in all: three against three. Only two of us would remain in the running.

The opposing team disappeared, hiding among some ruins that had suddenly appeared. I got to my feet and looked around, fascinated. We were still in an arena, but this time it was on Earth: an underground level of the Colosseum in Rome. The crowds roared, hungry to see us do battle. This time there were no virtual realities to hide us from them, though the glass muffled their cheers. Our teams' charts became visible on the surface of the dome. I made my way through the ruins, hiding myself behind the tall walls of the ancient corridors. I touched one of them. The gladiators' blood seemed to pulse in the blocks of ancient stone. Now I was one of them.

Something captured my attention. A lioness emerged from a cage, its head low, and slowly crept toward me. I had slain far more ferocious creatures.

"Heeeere, kitty kitty kitty," I murmured, my muscles tensed.

In reply, the feline opened its enormous jaws wide. I gaped at its many rows of teeth. There wasn't even room in its mouth to devour its prey unless it was already torn into tiny pieces. It was definitely a very unusual lioness.

With a roar, it swiped at me with its giant paw and pounced, knocking me to the ground. I struggled to keep it away as it offered me a close-up of its entire mouth full of teeth. "I didn't come this far just to get torn apart by a she-cat," I warned it. Somehow I managed to reach my knife and stab it between the eyes, but the blade shattered into a thousand pieces when it hit its skin. "Wow, are you hard-headed," I joked. "Not as much as me, though." I bit down on its jugular, squeezing my teeth shut.

The beast instantly froze, gripped with convulsions. I quickly rolled away before the electric charge could knock me out. "I didn't know I had such a shocking bite."

"Biting's against the rules, didn't you know that?"

I pulled myself out from under the feline, which had slumped on top of me, lifeless. *I knew that voice.* It was Faust, his stun gun still pointed at the lioness. For a second I'd hoped the Witch had rewarded me with a superpower, but now I saw it hadn't been my bite that had electrocuted the beast. Faust laughed, seeing the disappointed look on my face.

"There's a rulebook?" I asked.

"It's one of those things they teach you in preschool. I guess you never went?" He held out his hand to help me up and I grabbed it. Faust was a good friend. We had often battled in the Opalion, but outside the Arena he had always proved to be an ally.

"Nice gadget," I said, pointing at his stun gun.

He showed it to me. It was large and streamlined. Its projectiles were positioned around it: glass capsules with lightning bolts inside them. Electric and lethal. "I'm the king of thunderstorms," he said, blowing across the muzzle of his weapon. "What have you got?"

I pulled out my arsenal. It took a while to show him all the weaponry. When I was done he whistled. "Watch out for metal detectors."

"Good advice."

Something landed on the wall above us. We spun around, weapons drawn. The enemy had been so fast that neither of us had seen him coming. In a flash he was behind us, pressing our own weapons against our backs.

"I would not do that again if I were you." His voice was deep, his accent ancient. I wondered how long he had been in Hell.

"No need to get your panties in a bunch, Amhir," Faust said, slowly turning around. "We're on the same side."

The man lowered the weapons and with a single movement returned them to us. "For now," he replied sternly. He
had dark skin and a crew cut. I remembered his chart. He
was the Champion sent in by Bathsheeva, the golden-eyed
warrior Witch.

"*For now,*" Faust mimicked him behind his back.

Laughing, I elbowed him. "Come on, let's go. If there's
one thing I've learned from playing video games it's that
you've got to keep moving forward if you want to track
down your opponents." We walked down the narrow corridors of the ancient arena like mice in a maze. The only way
out was death. The death of all but one of us.

The Champions were stronger than any Souls I'd faced
in Hell. Not only because they were Subterraneans but also
because they'd all been trained—and for a lot longer than
me. Still, I was confident. Anyone who tried to come
between me and Stella, I would kick their ass.

A cable shot past me and coiled around Amhir's ankle.
It yanked him off his feet and dragged him away. I looked
around, disoriented. It had all happened so fast I didn't even
know where it had come from. Amhir, however, wasn't
about to be defeated so easily. He grabbed the metal line
and tried to break it. When that didn't work he pulled out a
large flamethrower. A spurt of flame burst from its barrel,
lighting everything up. The cable snapped and he somersaulted backwards, landing in perfect balance. The other
three Champions, our opponents, climbed over the walls of
the ancient arena and leapt down.

Amhir turned to face them, a threatening look in his eye.
"Time for a barbecue," he said, pulling the trigger on his

flamethrower, "and I want meat." He directed the flames at the three soldiers, but one of them blocked the oncoming fire with ice.

Faust brandished his gun, the lightning bolts dancing inside the bullets anxious to unleash a firestorm.

I pulled out my machine gun, sure there was still some ammo left . . . well, pretty sure. "And I thought *I* had cool weapons."

Faust laughed. "It's not the weapon that counts, my friend. It's how you use it." He fired silent shots toward the stream of ice, which shattered into a thousand pieces. Now unhindered, Amhir's fire spread out, driving our adversaries back against a stone wall. "Okay, the weapon counts too," he said, shrugging.

I shook my head and followed him, running toward the three Champions. Each of us aimed at one adversary. The blow had left them dazed, but they too had their Amìshas' blood in their veins. Underestimating them would be a mistake.

They all got up at the same time, like marionettes. But then again, we were all puppets. That was partly why I was fighting: to finally cut the strings that made me the Witches' slave.

Faust took aim at the tattooed Viking with the blond beard. I remembered his chart: his name was Bohr and he was battling for Zafirah, the Witch with violet eyes.

Assin and I stared each other down. He was my sole objective: the Subterranean who had killed me on Earth. An even worse enemy than the Witches. I would make sure he never made it to the next level. I wasn't about to give him the satisfaction of chalking up another victory against me.

I launched my attack, but Misha the Russian stepped between us, blocking my way. It was Amhir who challenged Assin instead. Whatever. If there was anyone who could keep him from leveling up, it was Amhir.

"Your race to glory has just ended, Champion." Misha spat the words out in his Russian accent while he brandished his heavy weaponry: jointed metal claws and a hook to gouge my eyes out.

"Didn't they ever trim your fingernails when you were little?" Dodging the claws, I jumped back, then swung the scythe and chopped off his fingers. "*Voilà*. Problem solved."

He screamed in rage and pain and his hook lodged in my side.

I cursed, gritting my teeth. As I readied myself to finish him off, a strange low-pitched noise echoed through the Arena. Another blast of the horn, grimmer than the ones before it. This time it wasn't announcing a victory; it was a death knell instead. The first player had been defeated.

We peered around, trying to understand what had happened. Amhir was on the ground. His limp body disintegrated and disappeared. He had left the level. Two of our adversaries ran off and Captain Hook followed them, depriving me of my revenge.

I couldn't believe Assin had defeated a fierce Champion like Amhir. Faust ran up to me, also shaken by what had happened. Not because we'd had a bond with Amhir, but because he'd had one of the highest scores. Amhir had been powerful, but Assin had eliminated him all the same. We needed to stay alert.

"Let's split up," I suggested to Faust. He nodded and disappeared among the ruins. I looked around and for the first time, surrounded by the ancient walls, I felt like a gladiator. I spun the knife in my hand, thinking of what Misha had said.

He'd been wrong. My race to glory had just begun.

GHOSTS IN THE MIND

I leaned against a wall and slid down to the ground, clenching my jaw against the pain in my side. That hooked bastard had dug a hole in my flesh. The scratches elsewhere on my body soon vanished but the wound was deep. I pulled off my armor, leaving my chest bare. Drops of sweat slid down my skin, setting my wounds aflame. At least the spectators watching me on the screens would be focused on how sexy I was shirtless rather than thinking about my weaknesses. I tensed my jaw and rested my head against the wall as the wound sealed up, burning even more. A small reward for my presumptuousness, like Kreeshna always said. I wondered if Stella was watching me.

"Drake!" My blood ran cold when I heard her voice. I shot to my feet and followed the echo, but came to a dead end. *"Drake! Help me, please!"*

I raced in the opposite direction, following the sound—

but ended up in another dead end. Confused, I looked around, my eyes narrowed. It was a trick. The Witches wanted to slow me down. While I was wasting time on their little mind games, the others were battling it out to clinch a place in the final round. I had to stay focused on my mission. Now that so few of the Witches were left, the competition was getting fiercer. There was no way for me to know what kind of moves they would come up with to annihilate me.

"Drake! I'm over here!"

Ignoring all logic, I raced toward her voice. "Stella!" Her name echoed off the ancient walls.

"Help me, please!"

I turned a corner and went stock-still at the sight of her. It was Stella, yes, but not the one from Hell. It was the Stella from my past, the one I had abandoned.

"Drake," she murmured, "help me."

Slowly I came closer. Her clothes were threadbare and torn, her skin covered with bruises, scratches, and burns. Who knew what she had been through in Hell. And it was all my fault.

"I'm here," I replied in a whisper. "I'm here now." With a frightened shake of her head, she raised her palm to keep me away. "Stella, it's me." Didn't she recognize me?

She let out an anguished shriek, her eyes suddenly filled with terror. I couldn't stand seeing her like this. I rushed to embrace her, but the moment I touched her she exploded into a million pieces, leaving me with a handful of ash. I staggered back. *What had I done to her?!* Her experience must have been atrocious. I would never forgive myself for abandoning her.

"Drake." This time her voice was barely a murmur.

I turned around and she was there again. A tear slowly trickled down her cheek. *"Don't leave me here alone. I'm afraid."*

A shiver ran down my spine at her ghastly whisper. "Stella," I said softly.

A patch of black blood appeared on her chest, quickly spreading as she fixed her terrified eyes on me. "It hurts!" she screamed.

Once again I ran to her, but her eyes changed, becoming cold and detached. They were the eyes of an Insane Soul, exactly what Stella had been turning into before I arrived. Refusing my help, she huddled in a niche in the wall, chewing on the hem of her dress.

"Stella, get hold of yourself. It's me. I'm here now."

"It's too late."

I turned toward the new voice. Toward the new Stella. This time I recognized her: it was the Stella who had risen from the ashes. *The one who wanted to kill me.* Her bow was drawn, the arrow aimed at me, just like at our first encounter in the Gluttons' cave.

"You're the cause of everything."

It was true. It was my fault Stella had become a ruthless assassin, unable to control her thirst for blood.

She released the arrow, but it didn't hit me. Instead, the young Stella crumpled to the ground. I ran to her. Blood gushed from her mouth. She tried to tell me something but before she had the chance she exploded into millions of pieces, making me shield my face.

I looked up. I was alone, but my remorse hadn't disappeared with the Stellas. To survive, she'd been forced to kill her own innocence, to become someone else. To become *something* else. Thanks to me, that innocent part of her had vanished forever.

"Drake!" Again her voice echoed through the Arena like an obsession.

I knew she wasn't really there. The Witches were putting my mental endurance to the test, trying to break me. Or maybe it was just a trick to slow me down.

"Drake, help me! Please."

I didn't hesitate a second. "Stella! Where are you?" I had to save her. I would never stop trying to save her. I threw myself to my knees and grabbed her hand before she could fall off the edge of a cliff that had just appeared.

"Don't abandon me again," she begged me.

A tear rolled down my cheek as I realized I would never stop feeling guilty about what I'd done to her, about everything she'd had to go through because of me.

"Drake, I don't want to be one of the Insane. Please, save me." My eyes widened. Her voice was like it used to be, exactly how I remembered it: free from all traces of Hell. Innocent.

"You broke her," Kahlena the warrior said. She was crouched atop a wall, enjoying the scene. "You'll never bring her back."

Her words were a stab to my heart. I looked at the hand I was gripping to keep Stella from falling into the void and finally understood.

"I don't want to bring her back." I released my grip and Stella's hand slipped from my fingers.

The remorse I felt for having left her had never ceased to haunt me, but there was one thing I didn't regret: the new Stella I'd met in Hell. Kahlena. I touched the strip of cloth tied around my arm, my heart full of her. I had to accept her. In her situation, many others would have died, or worse. She, instead, had been reborn by becoming stronger, more determined. Hell had put her to the test and revealed her true soul. It was the soul of a warrior, and I was proud of it.

I stood up and Kahlena also disappeared. If all this had been yet another of the Witches' trials designed to distract me from my goal, I must have passed the test by banishing the phantoms trapped in my mind.

I felt stronger. Freer.

All at once something gripped my neck and forced me to the ground. I thrashed my legs, trying to break free, my hands clutching at the steel cords. I recognized the weapon, one of the two large, lethal yo-yos with metal cords the Viking Bohr was skilled at using. It was he who had lassoed Amhir.

The wire went slack and retracted. I remained on the ground while the wound Bohr had just inflicted on me healed. The Viking stood above me. "Want to play with me for a while?" he asked with a smirk, making his deadly toys dance.

I rolled over to avoid the spinning blades and leapt to my feet. "Why not? Let's see what you can do with your little circus tricks."

He whipped a yo-yo at me, but I was faster and back-flipped off the wall, landing on the ground amid the shower of sparks the lethal yo-yo had struck off the stone. Yo-yo-man launched a second attack, the sparkling spheres slicing through the air, longing to taste my flesh. I studied his movements, waiting for the right time to counterattack.

"I like this game," I said, brandishing my scythe, "but I'm getting kind of tired of it." I intercepted the trajectory of the metal cords and with a flick of my wrist coiled the yo-yos around the scythe's handle, leaving Bohr unarmed.

He stared at me in shock. I could be fast too. He tried to attack me but I dodged his punch and slammed him into the wall with a kick. Quick as lightning, I slid across the ground and delivered a right hook that missed his throat by an inch. "Sorry, I'm kind of in a hurry."

He laughed, his expression mocking. "You've failed."

The horn of death sounded in the Arena as blood began to trickle from his throat.

"I never fail." The crescent blade in my glove retracted as swiftly and silently as it had appeared.

Bohr crumpled to his knees and vanished. My lethal blow had eliminated him from the game, but he wasn't really dead. Only the two Champions in the final round would truly put their lives at stake. And I was going to be one of them.

29

LEVEL TWO

Four of us were left.

Unfortunately, the Viking's weapons disappeared along with him before I could get my hands on them. Oh well. I would get by without his deadly yo-yos. Now all I had to do was find the next Champion to defeat.

I wandered among the ancient stone walls. The section where I was had once been the underground level of the Colosseum, where the gladiators prepared to make their entrance into the arena. Back then, a wooden platform covered with dirt had rested atop the now-uncovered stone walls. That had been the battlefield. It was the Witches who had brought the gladiator games to Earth, a primitive version of the Opalions that mortals called *munera*.

A stream of water flowed from a small fountain. I scooped some up in my cupped hands and the liquid turned orange. Challenging fate, I drank deep. Not bad. Tasted like an energy drink. Maybe it would give me superpowers. I stared at my fists but nothing happened.

Something darted past underground and before I knew it a stone wall right in front of me collapsed, followed by another one that almost crushed me. The earth beneath my feet lurched and I fell. It was as though someone had stuck out their foot and tripped me. What was going on?

"Drake!" Faust rushed toward me, his tone urgent. "Did you see it too?"

"See what?"

The thing darted by underground again. Whatever it was, it was enormous.

"That!" he shouted as a beast burst through the earth, its fangs open. Faust and I dove to the ground to avoid ending up in its belly. "Run!"

"What the hell is it?" I shouted as we fled. The beast chased us with its enormous head and sharp teeth. It was like the mutant offspring of a dragon and a snake.

"How should I know? All I know is that it wants to eat us!"

The beast slithered after us like a possessed serpent. Escaping would be no easy feat, with the walls crashing down all around us. From time to time it reared up and dove back down into the ground like a worm.

All at once it stopped and everything went quiet.

Something flashed above us. We both looked up at the dome. Electrical charges were snaking across it like lightning bolts in a storm.

"What's going on?" I murmured.

"Nothing good, I imagine."

The charts of the six Champions competing in level two suddenly appeared on the dome like holograms on a screen. Two of them exploded and Faust and I took shelter from the shower of shards. The four remaining charts were scrambled and then lined up in a single row. The message was clear: no more teams. The rules had just changed. I clenched my fists but didn't turn to look at Faust. We had both known the time would come when only one of us would triumph.

The beast emerged from the ground again and I instinctively whipped out my scythe, injuring its tail. An infernal shriek echoed through the Arena as it disappeared beneath the surface again.

Faust and I stood back to back, on our guard.

"Wasn't this supposed to be a challenge among Champions?" I whispered, trying not to make too much noise.

"It still is. The Witches like to have fun, that's all."

I shrugged. "The greater the difficulty, the greater the glory."

"Quoting Cicero won't help you level up," he said with a derisive laugh.

What happened next was so fast neither of us saw it coming. The earth beneath our feet erupted and I found myself hurled upwards. I came crashing down, the ground shaking from the impact. Or maybe it was my bones that shook. It was like falling off the Empire State Building. Every part of my body felt broken. Aching, I tried to get up. Faust came over to me. "Do I at least look sexy?" I asked him. The pain was crushing me like a boulder.

Faust grinned. "Yeah, I was just about to ask you to marry me."

I coughed and managed to haul myself to my feet. "Sorry, I'm already taken."

The walls around us exploded from the fury of the beast, which charged me again. It opened its jaws and I realized I had no way out. It was going to devour me.

All at once Faust pushed me out of the way. The serpent-dragon sank its teeth into him instead.

"No!" I screamed, running to the spot where he lay as the beast slithered back into the ground. I coughed again, my bones still feeling broken. Faust, though, was in far worse shape than me. His belly had been slashed open. He would never make it. "What were you thinking, dumbass?" I shouted at him. We were opponents. He wasn't supposed to sacrifice himself for me.

"You're my fiancé, don't you remember?" He laughed and blood trickled down his chin.

"You freaking idiot, you shouldn't have eliminated yourself for me."

"Conceited as always. I didn't do it for you." He motioned me closer and I leaned over him. "It wasn't my decision. This is your chance. Don't waste it." He winked at me and then vanished, exploding as the horn blared.

"Take care of Stella while I'm gone," I murmured to the wind.

Faust hadn't been able to give me the details of the decision he'd mentioned, but the message was clear: it had been his Amìsha who had given him that order. It certainly hadn't been to help me; rather, it showed she cared more about her

Champion than glory. Sacrificing him for a game would have been a waste. The other Witches didn't seem to understand that, blinded as they were by the infamous glory to which they aspired. That was why Faust's Amisha had kept him out of the final level, where leaving the game meant ending up in Oblivion.

This time I had managed to get my hands on Faust's gun before it vanished with him.

The ground shook again, warning me of the beast's return. I turned, my eyes aflame. The second it emerged I fired nonstop while striding toward it. It shrieked and writhed from the electric shocks. The thunderbolts enveloped it like a deadly vortex, but I didn't stop. I flung myself to the ground to dodge its attack, and when it charged me again, I threw myself on top of it, grabbing hold of the small horns on its head. The electrical current spread through me, making me grit my teeth. I didn't care. I wasn't letting go. The objective of the trial wasn't to kill the beast. I'd realized that when our charts appeared on the dome: the last category without a score was *physical endurance*. All I had to do was resist longer than the others.

"Want to take me for a spin, you big brute?"

It screeched and took me at my word, rearing up and preparing to disappear underground with me riding on its back.

"Shit."

I held on tight, bracing for impact, but the ground turned into water and the beast dragged me down into its depths. I clung to it with all my might, disoriented. Was it hoping to drown me? Normally I didn't need to breathe, but when I felt the water closing my throat I realized that things were different for my character in this game.

I pulled out my dagger and stabbed the serpent-dragon in the ear. It bucked and I lost my grip on it. I hung onto the dagger for dear life as the animal streaked upward through the water. We broke the surface and with a lurch the beast freed itself, flinging me onto a rock.

The cheers from the crowds filled my ears. I looked around, catching my breath. The dome separating us from the spectators had disappeared. I could even see the Witches peering down at us from above like vultures, waiting for the last of us to fall.

The entire Arena was filled with water. I could see the other two Champions who had earlier been hidden by the walls of the ancient Colosseum also clinging to the rocks.

Three of us were left. The first to admit defeat would send the other two to the final round. We looked at each other. Who among the three of us would be the last man standing?

The sea serpent attacked again. I abandoned the rock and jumped onto a floating metal disk. There were lots of them, and I discovered they formed a path, which I followed, teetering with every step, until I finally reached the center of the Arena.

Wrong move. The water receded all at once, sending me and my two opponents tumbling to the ground. I glared at Assin, forcing down the hatred I harbored for him. I had to stay focused.

Suddenly I heard the roar of water. I sprang to my feet. It was a shock when I looked around to see the Arena filling with water again. It stopped, leaving a straight strip of dry land.

"Ah. Something biblical. I should have expected it," I murmured, glancing up at the Stage Director. Now that we were at the bottom of the Arena-sea she was so high up she looked like a drop of black blood in the twilight.

Assin raced toward one of the rocks and I realized it would be a good idea to do the same. A split second later, the water came crashing down onto the strip of land. I would never reach the nearest rock in time so I leapt onto a metal disk an instant before the blast hit me. It wasn't easy to keep a firm grip with the waves knocking me every which way like savage beasts determined to do me in. *I had to hold on.* At least until one of the others gave up. At that point there would only be two of us, and we would have earned our spots in the final round.

But the Witches had other plans for me.

The monster surfaced again, veered, and rammed me. My mouth filled with water and I lost my hold on the disk. I rose to the surface, treading water and thrashing around for something to cling to. The Russian Champion was in trouble too. The serpent burst up between us like a giant waterspout, then crashed down onto the surface of the sea again. The impact raised a wall of water that risked drowning us all. I ended up right in the middle of the towering waves and was sucked down into a whirlpool. As my head went under, I saw Misha grab hold of a disk and save himself.

I had failed.

Below the surface everything was calm. I let the tranquility cradle me as I waited for the horn of death to sound for me. I closed my eyes and Stella's image filled my mind.

A second later I snapped them open, shaking myself out of my daze. I might be defeated, but it certainly wouldn't be by choice. I struggled to resurface before it was too late. Something grabbed my arm and dragged me up as I heard the sound of the horn.

Had I lost? Still dazed, I saw Misha being sheared in two by the beast.

I was still in the game.

I turned toward the hand that had saved me. Assin smiled at me, amused. "I didn't want you to miss the final round."

Misha and I had had the same chances of dying, but Assin had chosen to save my life. There could be only one reason: this way he could finally *really* kill me.

The water drained away, taking with it the beast, which disappeared into the floor of the Arena. The Empress's voice filled the silence. *"Level two complete."*

All that remained was the final trial. The trial of strength.

The one where you either lived or died.

30

LIKE THE FIRST TIME

It was worse than an earthquake. It's not easy to keep your balance when an arena transforms beneath your feet. The entire battlefield detached itself from its foundations and levitated into the air like an uprooted plant.

Something was happening below us. I saw it on the screens, which now formed a halo suspended over the Arena. The ground folded in on itself, becoming a silver cube. Each of its six sides had a different surface: one was covered with burning coals, another with sharp spikes, while still another dripped with black oil. Or was it demon blood?

The worst part, though, was the dark vortex materializing beneath the cube: Oblivion, the only realm capable of annihilating a Subterranean's soul for all eternity.

"You have been struck, stabbed, deceived." The Empress's voice filled the amphitheater, capturing Assin's and my attention. The Damned in the stands obediently fell silent. "You have demonstrated your endurance by rising up again after each defeat. Your bravery has led you here. Now you will be called upon to test your strength in the player-versus-player arena." The word *Strength* began to flash on the screen. "Prepare yourselves for the final great challenge that only one of you will survive. Fight, Champions. Battle to achieve victory in the final round . . . or die trying."

The audience burst into excited whistles and cheers—ogres, Damned Souls, and deformed beasts that had all come to witness one of the Champions being slain. I forced myself to look away from the screen and focus on my opponent.

A tingle ran through my fingers as a new suit of armor, complete with helmet, formed over me. I stared at my arms, amazed. Though you couldn't tell from the look of it, it was digital. That was why it was so light.

I'd played too many video games not to feel like I was in one of them. I had ventured through Hell to reach the Castle and save my princess. Kreeshna was right: my challenges had begun long ago. What I hadn't realized was that I was only a pawn, a character she had developed battle by battle, forging and sharpening my abilities. All that was left now was the final match, the one inside the Castle. Luckily for me, I was good at PvP games. It wouldn't be so different from playing Mortal Kombat except for the pain, the wounds, and the very real risk of ending up in Oblivion.

Our charts were displayed side by side on the screen: *Assin vs. Drake.* Two of us were left. The bravest, the cleverest, the toughest. Which of us would prove to be the strongest?

With his new helmet on, all I could see were my opponent's eyes. Fine. First thing I would do was gouge them out.

"We meet again," he said, an evil look in his eye.

I smiled, ready to take him on. "Assin. Is that your name? I bet that's short for 'Assassin.'"

"That's the short *and* the long of it." He thrust his arms forward and two swords shot out from his wrists. I dodged them just in time, sliding across the ground on my knees.

Something glinted on my arm. The armor. It wasn't only for protection, it was a virtual weapon. I tried to figure out how the tiles spinning around my forearm worked. They were digital buttons. I pressed one and my arm transformed, lengthening into a giant sickle. A heavy chain dangled from the tip of it, ending in a mace. Version 2.0 of my old weapon.

"This gear ain't bad," I said to myself. My new toy was kind of like a kusarigama, a ninja weapon I had often used in video games. I heard my enemy approaching from behind, spun around, and swung the mace at him. The chain wrapped around his neck several times, pulling me toward him. I leapt onto his back. "We'll see which one of us is the assassin this time." I was determined to finish what he had started back on Earth.

Assin broke free and came at me with both swords. I had waited a lifetime for this moment. I hadn't been sure I would ever find the Subterranean who had killed me, but the Witches were capricious; for reasons of their own, they were offering me the chance to avenge myself. It was an opportunity I wasn't going to miss.

"You should be thanking me," he said. Sparks flew from

our metal weapons as we took turns delivering brutal blows. "If I hadn't sent you down here, you never would've been reunited with your lovely lady."

Maybe so, but the circumstances weren't exactly the ones under which I would have chosen to find her again. Both our lives depended on this tournament. *They depended on me.* Maybe it would have been better if I hadn't found her again. At least she would be back in her cave, safe.

"I'll thank you if you help me get all this over with quickly. That way I can get back to her." I pressed another button and a harpoon attached to a chain shot from my arm like a missile. The audience gasped when it lodged in Assin's helmet. The blow left him dazed but he stayed on his feet. Steam rose from his armor. Small, pointed icicles formed all over its surface before continuing up the harpoon. The whole chain froze.

"Sorry," he shot back, "I'm not about to do you any favors. If you want victory, you'll have to earn it." With a jerk of his arm, he shattered my weapon into a thousand pieces. "May the best man win. That is: me." The darts of ice obeyed his command and flew toward me.

"Don't count on it." I raised my arms to protect myself and a metal shield took shape from my armor, absorbing the impact of the ice darts, which was so powerful it pushed me to my knees. When I stood up again to face my opponent the shield withdrew. "This gear is freaking awesome!" I marveled, noting how the pixels joined together, molding themselves around me. "Let's see what else it can do." I ran my hand over my chest in search of more buttons. Finding one, I pressed it, and an electric charge ran through me from head to toe. I watched as miniature bolts of lightning shot from my fingertips, reminding me of the gun I had taken from Faust. It was then that I understood: our armor integrated and amplified the powers of the weapons we'd managed to collect over the course of the game. *I* was the lightning now.

Assin jumped aside when I hurled the first bolt at him, followed closely by another. Inside me, I could feel the storm quivering, longing to surge and strike. Destroy. Burn. I hit him with another lightning bolt and he whirled through the air, crashing to the ground a good distance away.

I closed in on him to strike the fatal blow. He was face-down on the ground. At first he showed no sign of life, but then his hand reached out and clasped me weakly by the ankle. I chuckled. He didn't even have the strength to hold on to me, let alone get back on his feet.

Ice condensed on his palm and melted into water, dampening my ankle. The shock was so powerful it sent me hurtling back, steam rising from my body. Lightning bolts and water didn't mix. I struggled to focus my eyes. We were both on the ground. The Witches wouldn't have a winner at all if we fried each other to death.

Was it my head that was spinning or were their thrones moving? Assin and I sat up, both gripped by the same doubt. It wasn't a hallucination. The Witches were circling the Arena. The surface beneath us trembled. The cube began to turn horizontally along with them. I quickly staggered to my feet as the Witches decided our fate. Their faces swirled around me, haunting my mind like ghosts. When their thrones stopped, the cube did too. The surface changed, turning to ice.

It finally dawned on me: it wasn't a cube. It was a die. The Witches were playing dice with us.

Assin laughed and drew strength from the ice. His entire suit of armor crystallized and a volley of razor-sharp ice darts came rushing at me. *If only I'd gotten the flamethrower from Amhir!*

I tried to activate my other weapons but the mechanism seemed to be damaged. Assin realized I was having difficulties and charged. Where the hell were my weapons? I blocked his attack with a roundhouse kick, and a circular blade formed around my body. It struck Assin hard, shattering his icy shell, then retracted as swiftly as the little crescent-shaped blade that had been concealed in my glove. Now I was the glove, and the blade was human-size.

A new layer of ice formed over my opponent. He stamped up to me and his head-butt sent me flying. I groaned from the mighty blow, but Assin didn't give me the chance to get up. Like a sledgehammer, his massive fist of ice smashed down, barely missing my head. I rolled away and something in my armor activated: rotating blades sheared through the ice all around me. *But I hadn't pressed anything. Not intentionally, at least.*

The sharp sound of ice cracking warned me just in time. I shot my javelin to the edge of the die just as the ice gave way beneath me, opening a chasm. I dragged myself out of danger using the chain, which had regenerated.

Assin charged at me, heedless of the ground's fragility.

Instead of avoiding the chasm like I had, he leapt into the air, front-flipped, and dove into it.

"What the fuck?" I retracted the chain and squatted to see what was down there. The crowd rooted for me to follow him. I didn't want to go inside the die but I had no choice. "Aw, to hell with it," I murmured a moment before diving in myself.

Assin welcomed me with a punch. It wasn't a punch of ice. His bare knuckles smashed into my jaw. I looked around as the audience continued to cheer. We were still in the Arena, but everything had changed. We had left the virtual reality scenario. No more armor. No digital weapons that materialized on command. Just him and me. Like the first time.

With a sneer, he dared me to come at him. I slugged him in the face and continued to attack him with punches and kicks, forcing him back. We were in the real Arena now, the real deal. The brutal one, where the only special effects were punches and blood. During my imprisonment in the Castle I'd spent much of my time battling in that same Arena, one Opalion after another. Now for the first time I was facing the final challenge against another Champion and actually trying to win.

"I don't need special weapons to fight you," I told him as I peppered him with punches.

Assin managed to pull away from my wrath and dove back into the die. I followed him through into the virtual reality and this time managed to dodge his attack. The shield on my arm reactivated, absorbing the blast from his laser gun. When it grew incandescent I tossed it aside.

The armor was certainly useful, but on the screens I was definitely hotter without a shirt on.

The nail gun. Obeying my wish, my gloves fired a shower of deadly nails at him. My opponent tried to take shelter but one of them sank into his tibia, making him double over in pain. As I closed in on him I noticed razor-sharp disks scattered on the icy ground. So I hadn't been firing nails after all. They were ninja stars.

Before I could reach him, he cut a hole in the ground with his laser, climbed in, and sealed the ice over him. *The bastard.* I rushed to the spot and stared at him through the window of ice. We were in the same position, on our hands and knees, trapped in two different worlds, but with one sole objective: to win the tournament. I pounded my fist against the ice and he smirked. He had gained enough time for his wound to heal.

Suddenly he vanished. I peered through the ice, but it had grown thick and I couldn't see all the way through to the other side. Where had he gone?

"Never turn your back on your enemy." Assin grabbed me from behind and hurled me away. He'd created another hole between the two dimensions. He proceeded to make another and another and yet another, reducing the surface of the die to Swiss cheese.

"Wanna play hide-and-seek, you bastard?" I dove into one of the holes but didn't stay long on the other side. I found him in another one of the holes and, clinging to the edge, threw myself on top of him.

All at once the ground tilted, jostling us like marionettes

in a puppet show. A knife shot out of my palm and I instinctively jammed it into the ice for a handhold.

It was the die. The Witches had begun to turn again on their platforms, and with them the huge die beneath us. I felt like I was on a spinning top. When it stopped moving and began to tilt, a terrible suspicion prompted me to move, and fast.

31

WIN OR DIE

The Witches were playing dice with our lives.

I dug a second dagger into the ice and scrambled upward for dear life. Until that moment the die had only moved horizontally, but now it had tilted dangerously upward. It was turning upside down, threatening to make us fall into empty space. I reached the edge and pulled myself up onto another side of the die, the one covered with black blood.

Not far away, I could see Assin. He was also exhausted after the grueling climb. I had to seize my chance. I slid down toward him and knocked him over.

My hand sank into the black slime and I felt it solidify beneath my fingers. "Fascinating," I murmured, studying the malleable substance. With a flick of my wrist I pulled a handful of it up into a pillar that glistened like black ice. No, not ice. Carbonado, the Witches' favorite diamond. The harpies wanted us Champions to be just like the cursed gem: cold, hard, deadly. I quickly surrounded Assin with a series of sharp pillars, sealing him into a cage. In response, he swung his unsheathed sword, shattering the bars of his cage into thousands of black shards that flew toward me. I raised a wall to shield myself and heard them crash against it.

Figures rose up out of the muck: an army forged by Assin, programmed to kill me. I lunged toward my adversary, reducing his soldiers to bits. "Sorry I broke your dollies," I said when I reached him. Hatred returned to burn in my veins. "Not even an entire army can keep me from killing you for what you did to me and my friends."

"I had nothing against you, you should know that. Once I'd taken your place, you were in the way, that's all."

"What did you do to my friends?!" I snarled, rushing at him. I would mix his red blood with the black slime and then I would turn him into a fossil.

"I blew the icy breath of death upon them, as I was ordered to."

I froze, my blood running cold. "You did *what?!*" I yelled. I couldn't bear the thought that he had harmed my friends. It had to be a lie, a trick to weaken me. "You're lying!"

"Someone died in that house, and I'm not talking about you," he said with a complacent smirk.

I was in shock. Had that bastard killed Gemma? Evan would never have let that happen. A supernatural strength surged up inside me. I charged him and a powerful energy burst from my palms, hurling him to the far end of the battlefield. I stared at my fists, feeling the power course through my veins. They sparkled orange, like the potion I'd drunk in the Arena. At the Castle Subterraneans weren't allowed to have powers, but during the Games it seemed we were.

"Come to think of it, since you're here it means they must've kicked your ass," I retorted. His sneer became a glower. "What's wrong, don't feel like smiling any more?" Even if Assin had managed to kill my brother's girlfriend, they had definitely made him pay for it. "My family must've punished you for your sins, but now it's my turn to take *my* revenge." I swept up the carbonado and it wound around his body, raising him up as though he were tied to a stake.

Just then the die moved, turning over again.

As I slid down I tried to grab hold of something, to shape handholds for myself, but the slime itself was oozing down the die, covering it like poisoned caramel on an apple.

The ropes of slime binding Assin's body kept him firmly rooted to the surface of the die, even though it was spinning, whereas I slid down its side, desperately grappling for something to hold onto. Beneath me, Oblivion beckoned, threatening to swallow me up. If I fell off, it was the end, the end for both me and Stella. I refused to give in.

The die tilted upwards, giving me a small respite, but I lost my grip and rolled down. As I fell, I snatched at one of the spikes covering the bottom of the die and clung to it with all my might. I had to hold on until the die stopped, but my chances weren't good, dangling over the void as I was. I looked at the strip of cloth Stella had tied around my arm. She was counting on me. I couldn't let her down. Somehow, I had to climb up to the top before Assin was declared the winner. The problem was I had no idea how to get there.

"What a thorny situation," I muttered, passing from one spike to the next. The entire surface was covered with them. I was happy the die hadn't stopped with that side up.

"The thorns hold the sweetest poison."

My head snapped toward the voice. *Assin.*

"How the hell—" My eyes bulged when his head appeared below the edge of the die, upside-down. How was he staying attached to the wall? "Did your armor come with a user's manual or what?"

His expression turned cutting. "I've come to finish what I started. This time I'm not giving you a hand."

Tightening my grip on the spikes, I swung my legs up and pinned his head between them. Assin pulled back in surprise but I clung tight and dragged him down. He tried to grab me but slipped and plunged into the void with a scream.

"Me neither," I shot back, watching him fall.

I heaved a long sigh. It wasn't over yet. I swung from one spike to the next, finally pushing myself up onto the vertical side of the die. There I made the welcome discovery that my gloves magically remained attached to its sheer wall. I climbed it easily.

My face filled the screens as I pulled myself up onto the top surface of the die. I raised my head, a look of triumph on my face. The entire Arena erupted in cheers for the new Champion. *Cheers for me.* I clenched my fists, staring at Kreeshna. I had won.

Pride filled her serpent-like eyes when the throne of her

last Sister descended and she remained. The final Witch in the game.

My eyes sought Stella among the crowd. It was over. At last, it was all over. Stella and I would be free to live in peace, hidden away in some little corner of Hell, holding each other close in our secret paradise.

I continued to carefully scan the crowd, but I couldn't find her. Where was she?

The end of the tournament had caused pandemonium among the Damned. No doubt countless bets had been won —and lost—with my victory. Nevertheless, the most coveted prize would be going to me and I couldn't wait to claim it.

The Arena came to rest on the ground with a thud, sealing off the abyss of death as the Damned went wild with excitement. That is, until they heard the Empress's voice.

"Silence!" As though she had cast a spell, stillness instantly fell over the stands. "It is time to applaud she who has earned this victory, our Sisterhood's beloved Kreeshna. Kneel before her!"

All obeyed as Kreeshna descended from her throne and strode toward me in the center of the Arena. A swarm of black butterflies fluttered in our direction. They danced around us and then came together to form the spiky crown.

"Let all those present revere the new Queen of the Dark Tournament, she who trained and guided her Champion to victory, vanquishing all her Sisters." Sophia shouted Kreeshna's name again and again, encouraging the Damned to follow suit.

I snorted. *Like she was the person who'd won it.*

An army of she-warriors marched toward us. Was Stella

among them? I struggled to spot her among the hundreds of faces, but Kreeshna grasped my hand and thrust it into the air, showing me off to the kingdom like her trophy.

"Drake Reeves," Sophia announced, but I didn't hear her. The voices in the Arena faded away as my eyes nervously surveyed the approaching she-warriors. The sound of their footsteps crowded my mind, drowning out even the clamor of the Damned. "You have valiantly battled fearsome adversaries," the Empress went on. "For your Amisha you have forged your glory. Henceforth you will forever live as her Champion."

I turned to Kreeshna, devastated by the proclamation. "What is she talking about?" She gave me an evil smile. "Hold on!" I protested. "I won. You've got to give me what I've earned!" The she-warriors surrounded me, blocking my path and keeping me at a distance from the new queen. "No . . ." I whispered desperately. *This wasn't really happening.* I looked for Stella among them, but my head began to reel.

Then I heard her voice in the distance. I spun around and saw her at the edge of the Arena. A group of Mizhyas put her in chains and dragged her away.

"Drake!!" Her desperate cry broke my heart in two.

"Stella!!" I tried to reach her, straining against the Mizhyas that held me back. I killed two of them, but a moment later the panthers streamed onto the field, snarling at me. The Mizhyas held me down. Their strength was no doubt enhanced by Kreeshna's powers, because I was unable to break free.

"Let me go!" I snarled, trying to wrench myself free. Why were they taking her away? "Kreeshnaaa!" I shouted the name with all the anguish of a man sentenced to death. After all, that was exactly what I was without Stella. "I didn't do all this just for your fucking glory!"

The Witch smiled. "But that's *exactly* what you did it for. That's what all our Champions do it for. Did you really think you would be given a reward different from what the others fought for? Don't worry. I'll reward you properly for your efforts."

"I'll never fuck you, you ugly snake!" I spat at her feet and the crowd let out an audible gasp. A Champion who spat at his queen after winning the crown for her wasn't something you saw every day. I knew Kreeshna would make me pay for the insult, but what else could she take from me that she hadn't already stolen?

"Oh yes you will, and I promise you'll like it."

I growled like a caged beast. If only I could free myself I would tear her heart out. "Where are they taking her?!"

"Where she won't jeopardize the bond between us. By winning for me you've signed her death sentence."

I staggered back in a state of shock that verged on madness. I had won the tournament but there was no winning against the Witch. "We had a deal," I said in a low, hoarse voice, utterly devastated.

"You should be more careful who you make deals with."

"I thought the word of a Witch meant something."

Kreeshna laughed. "Not mine. Did you really think I would give you up after seeing you battle so ardently for me?"

Rage flooded my chest. "I've never battled for you!"

"Oh yes you have. You received my blood within you.

You defeated eight opponents, the most valiant Champions in all Hell. You made me Queen of the Dark Tournament. For a thousand years I'll bear the title—and I owe it all to you."

"Then let us go. You got what you wanted."

"A queen can't lose her most intrepid Champion. Don't you realize that?"

"I'll be your Champion, then, but let Stella go. Please."

"Your pretty little friend served her purpose, but now she's only a hindrance. As long as she's alive, part of her will forever haunt your dreams. You need to be devoted to me, body, heart, and soul. No one must ever come between us."

"That's never going to happen! Let her go and I swear she'll be dead to me."

"Too late. I've already seen to that."

As if on cue, Stella's face filled the screens, her eyes bulging as a blade stabbed her in the back.

"Nooooo!!" I shrieked. My head spun and my legs went numb. I crumpled to my knees, gripping the earth. My sight blurred with tears, I barely saw Kreeshna's feet approaching me.

"Bind him," she ordered. The Mizhyas obeyed. "Losing her now will seem like the end of the world to you, but it will pass. Time and my lymphe will make you forget her completely, and together you and I will be unstoppable. Until that happens, as long as the slightest trace of her still pollutes your mind, you'll be locked up. It may take days, years, even centuries. That's up to you. It makes no difference to me."

"It's not fair," I whispered with my last remaining strength. Or maybe I only thought it.

"This is Hell. What did you expect?" Kreeshna turned her back on me.

I wished I could rip that smug smile off her face. With one last supreme effort, I managed to break free, but before I could reach her a panther pinned me to the ground, its claws sinking into my flesh. The poison rapidly entered my bloodstream. I let myself be dragged away, my mind lost in Stella's desperate eyes as they'd carried her off in chains and I'd done nothing.

Kreeshna was wrong. Nothing would make me forget her. Not even a thousand centuries. Those eyes would haunt my dreams for all eternity.

I succumbed to the poison and every trace of light faded, both outside and inside of me.

I had killed my Stella.

32

THE PHANTOM DEATH

I moaned as I came to. I was lying on a cold surface. The poison's effect was wearing off and the memories came flooding back. I had learned a bitter truth: there was no winning in Hell. My armor had vanished, leaving me clad only in my pants, my body covered with wounds. The most painful one, though, was in my heart. I had killed Stella.

How I longed to go back and undo everything. I wished I'd stayed in the Castle and never gone out looking for her. That way she would have been safe. Instead I'd condemned her to die. Stella hadn't needed me. I was the one who had needed her.

I'd battled, thinking I could save her, but the only way to do that would have been to lose to Assin. Another of the Witch's tricks, the reason Kreeshna had recruited her as a Mizhya. If I'd lost and been consigned to Oblivion, Stella would have remained in her service. That was why they had waited for my victory before arresting her. It wouldn't have made sense for Kreeshna to lose us both. The real challenge had been between Stella and me: Mizhya versus Champion. The bitterest and most painful of victories.

"Dark Tournament" was a perfect name for it, as dark as my grieving heart. I hadn't even been allowed to say goodbye to her . . .

Sophia had known that our stolen moment together before the final challenge would be our last. No matter how the tournament had ended, as of that moment we would never be together again. All that was left to me now was the sound of her desperate cry when she'd called my name. My eyes filled with tears at the memory of the blade sinking into her. I hadn't protected her.

The door creaked open and someone slipped inside. Without thinking I shot to my feet and shoved whoever it was against the wall. When I saw it was Khetra, I eased my grip, but tightened it again a second later. She was one of them.

"I have no wounds that you can heal, Mizhya," I growled into her face. She had always been there when I came to after an Opalion. Those harpies, the Witches, always wanted their warriors in top shape.

Her hand stroked my face, lingering on the cuts. "This time I'm not here for that."

"Whatever it is you want from me, you're not going to get it." I grabbed her hand and shoved her away.

She took the rejection in stride and smiled. "As full of yourself as always. Deep down that's why I like you so much."

I moved close to her and jabbed my finger in her face. "I trusted you. I thought you were helping me escape, but it was part of Kreeshna's plan all along."

"I didn't want to do it, but what I want matters nothing here. Subjugating yourself means giving yourself up."

"A shitty deal, if you ask me."

"You were fine with it too until not long ago." She rested her hand on my chest and I felt something cold in her palm. "Everyone needs redemption, Drake. Even the Damned." I closed my fingers around the pointy object and she pulled her hood over her head. "This is mine."

"What about mine, then?" I stopped her before she could leave the cell. "What about my redemption?"

"Go get it. You've earned it." Khetra turned and disappeared through the door.

"What does that mean?" I held up my hands in confusion, but she was gone. Only then did I notice what I was holding: a key. Did she want to help me run away again? Escaping from there would be impossible.

I went to the door of the cell, but discovered she had left it open. Cautiously, I peered out. Why would Khetra want to help me? Was it another trap? I stared at the key. What use was it, if the cell door was already open? Unless—

Stella. Maybe she was still alive. *She* was my redemption. That was what Khetra had been trying to tell me. Clinging to my new hope, I rushed down the corridor. They had stabbed Stella in the back but she hadn't disintegrated. Maybe I was still in time to say goodbye to her. Kreeshna had promised she would die and I knew she would see it through to the end, but if Stella was still alive I wanted to spend one last night next to her.

I searched all the dungeons. I had to find her and protect her with my own life. This time their blade would have to pass through me before it reached her. By getting rid of Stella the Witch thought she could have me, but that would never happen. Kreeshna wouldn't have that victory too, because I would die along with Stella.

I checked the umpteenth cell, but it was empty. They were all empty. Had they already disintegrated her? Or maybe it had just been an illusion.

"Drake!" A whisper behind me sent a jolt through my heart.

I spun around and there she was, clinging to the bars of a tiny cell. Was it a hallucination? An effect of the poison still circulating in my bloodstream? I pressed myself against the metal bars, yearning to squeeze her hands, so small, so cold.

"Drake," she whispered again. Her eyes brimmed with tears that overflowed and streamed down her face.

I brushed them away, unable to bear the sight of her weeping. "I thought they killed you." I gripped her hands in mine.

"I could never die without seeing you again first. That hope was what kept me alive in the Copse all that time."

Her confession made something inside me snap, and a tear coursed down my cheek. I rested my forehead at the height of hers on the other side of the bars. "Stubborn as always," I joked.

She laughed through the tears. I'd never known anyone with a spirit as strong as hers.

"Wait!" I slid the key into the lock and she pulled back in surprise.

"You have the key?!" she exclaimed. "How did——"

I pressed my lips against hers, cutting her off. All I wanted was to kiss her. Nothing mattered more than the warmth only she could give me. I wanted it to be my last memory when I closed my eyes before dying. I could never bear to lose her again. The first time had been devastating and I'd never recovered from it. This time I would choose to die with her. No longer would I subject myself to Kreeshna's rules. If she killed Stella, both of us would die.

I squeezed my eyes shut. The idea of losing her was unthinkable now after everything I'd done to save her. But there was no escaping from the Castle. My only consolation was that during our final moments we would be together at last.

The wound in her chest was deep. They had run her through with a sword, but it was already closing. When it came to blades, the only way to definitively destroy a Damned Soul was to stab him or her below the ear, in the spot where the blood flowed through the carotid artery. How long did we have before the Witches came to deal her the final blow?

"I'm sorry," I murmured, resting my forehead against hers. A tear slid down my face, cold and solitary like the death that awaited us.

"Everything is different now that you're here," she whispered against my lips.

"If only I hadn't gone out looking for you—" It was all my fault.

She shook her head. "If you hadn't, you wouldn't be the reckless fool who made me fall in love with him twice."

"When was the second?" I asked, repeating the question she had asked me back in the cave.

"When I shot you with that arrow, isn't it obvious?"

I smiled, pressing my forehead against hers. "Your way to claim me, I suppose."

She smiled back. "In a way."

"I knew that watching me in the Arena would get you all hot and bothered."

She punched me in the shoulder. Seeing her smile tore my heart into a thousand pieces. I couldn't let them kill her. But how could I prevent it?

For the Witches, Stella was simply one of the countless Souls in Hell. For me, she was my heaven. I gazed into her eyes for a long time while I considered a crazy new plan.

"Screw it!" I had to get her out of there. I grabbed her hand and pulled her toward the cell door, but she stopped me.

"Drake, wait!"

I turned to look at her, my voice tense. "We don't have much time. I've got to get you out of the Castle. They won't go out looking for you if I stay here to stop them."

"No! I'm not leaving you. We'll never get out of here alive, not like this."

"We have to at least try."

Her eyes locked on mine, she pulled something out of

her pocket. "I didn't say we wouldn't." Opening her palm, she revealed a vial full of black liquid.

"What's that?"

"It's a death serum."

That was just like Stella. Like me, she would rather kill herself than let the Witches win. "This is no time to play the martyr. If there's even the slightest chance, I'm getting you to safety."

"This," she insisted, holding up the vial, "will get us out of the Castle."

"Alive or dead? The name's not very encouraging."

"Both." She took a sip of it, her eyes fixed on me, then handed me the vial. "Trust me."

Our eyes didn't leave each other for an instant. I had no idea what she meant to do, but I trusted her. Maybe it was our last moment together. Not wanting to ruin it with words, I planted a desperate kiss on her mouth and gulped down the rest of the liquid.

The room began to spin and I squeezed my eyes shut. Not even Dakor poison had ever made me so dizzy. I tried to cling to something but felt myself falling. Stella grabbed my arm as the world came to a halt. Funny, I could have sworn I'd fallen but I was still on my feet.

I struggled to focus my eyes. I couldn't believe what I was seeing: another me lay on the ground, alongside a clone of Stella. "Who the hell are they?"

"Our only chance of getting out of here."

The sound of footsteps running in our direction put us both on guard. Seconds later the she-warriors burst into the cell. I clutched Stella's hand and protectively stepped in front of her.

"Kreeshna's not going to like this," Lenora said in a low voice, staring at the two corpses.

My eyes met Stella's, astonished. *They couldn't see us.* She smiled and whispered, "In just a few minutes, my body will explode into a cloud of ash and yours will vanish into Oblivion, like all the Subterraneans when they die." I stared at her, barely able to comprehend what she was saying.

"Now," she murmured. I nodded and led her out of the cell. We raced through the Castle, looking for a way out. Witches, Subterraneans, and she-warriors passed us but none saw us.

"How do we get out?" I didn't want to have to climb down the tower wall again.

Stella said nothing, just smiled mischievously and pulled me down a corridor. We came out of a door into the Arena, where we joined a throng of Damned Souls streaming out of the opened Castle gates. I turned to her. "Of course! I'd forgotten Sophia opens the Castle gates on Opalion and tournament days."

The cool air filled my lungs. I'd thought the Castle walls would be my tomb, the very walls that had once protected me from the dangers of Hell. Now I couldn't be happier to leave it far behind and plunge into the Copse.

I had promised myself I would save Stella, but once again she had been the one to save me. My little she-warrior.

"We'd better hurry," she whispered. "Let's get away from here before the effect wears off."

"What happened back there? Where did you find that stuff?" I asked, once we were in the safety of the trees.

"It's called the 'phantom death' because an infinitesimal part of you is sacrificed to save the rest."

I looked at my hands. It seemed like nothing had changed, but we had managed to get out without anyone seeing us. The Witches hadn't even detected our thoughts.

She answered my unspoken doubts. "They won't come looking for us. Our existence, the traces we left in their minds, remained in that prison cell. The Witches used to grant this serum to powerful mortals who'd been condemned to death—in exchange for their souls."

"So they went from one prison to another," I said. "Where'd you get it?"

"It turns out that being a Mizhya has its advantages."

"My little thief." I smiled and pulled her to me.

"We'll be safe now. As long as they never find us, of course."

My spirits sank at the thought. "What do we do now?"

"We've got to keep walking. Pretty soon our bodies will become visible again."

"Your cave isn't safe any more," I reminded her, feeling guilty for having deprived her of it.

Stella didn't seem at all upset. "We're not going back to the cave." She smiled at me and I frowned. A sparkle lit up her eyes. "The serum isn't the only thing I found."

"What else, then?"

Her hand slid into mine. "I know how to get out of Hell."

Drake and Stella's story continues in…
ROGUE ARENA

Text **AMORE** to 77948 to get new release alerts from me!
(US Only).
If you prefer emails, join my List of Readers at
www.ElisaSAmore.com/Vip-List.
I'd love to have you in my lists and I'll send you a message
when my next book comes out.

ALSO BY ELISA S. AMORE

If you enjoyed Drake's adventure in DARK TOURNAMENT, find out much more about him and his Subterranean brothers in the TOUCHED saga, which tells the story of Evan and Gemma. Evan is an Angel Death and Gemma is the mortal girl he's been ordered to kill. Read the gripping story of their journey Through Heaven and Hell to protect their love.

TOUCHED SAGA READING ORDER:

Touched: The Caress Of Fate

Unfaithful: The Deception of Night

Brokenhearted: The Power of Darkness

Expiation: The Whisper of Death

BOX SET: The Complete Series

SHORT STORIES (no reading order required):

The Mark Of Fate: Evan's Prequel

The Shadow of Fate: Gemma's Prequel

The *Touched* saga is available in ebook, paperback and audio.

ELISA S. AMORE

Elisa S. Amore is the number-one bestselling author of the paranormal romance saga *Touched*.

Vanity Fair Italy called her "the undisputed queen of romantic fantasy." After the success of Touched, she produced the audio version of the saga featuring Hollywood star Matt Lanter (*90210, Timeless, Star Wars*) and Disney actress Emma Galvin, narrator of *Twilight* and *Divergent*. Elisa is now a full-time writer of young adult fantasy. She's wild about pizza and also loves traveling, which she calls a source of constant inspiration. With her successful series about life and death, Heaven and Hell, she has built a loyal fanbase on social media that continues to grow, and has quickly become a favorite author for thousands of readers in the U.S.

Visit Elisa S. Amore's website and join her List of Readers at www.ElisaSAmore.com/Vip-List.

Find Elisa S. Amore on:

facebook.com/eli.amore

twitter.com/ElisaSAmore

instagram.com/eli.amore

Printed in Great Britain
by Amazon